OUT OF THIS WORLD LOVER

D1561947

OTHER ELLORA'S CAVE ANTHOLOGIES
AVAILABLE FROM POCKET BOOKS

BAD GIRLS HAVE MORE FUN
by Arianna Hart, Ann Vremont, & Jan Springer

ON SANTA'S NAUGHTY LIST
by Shelby Reed, Lacey Alexander, & Melanie Blazer

ASKING FOR IT
by Kit Tunstall, Joanna Wylde, & Elisa Adams

A HOT MAN IS THE BEST REVENGE
by Shiloh Walker, Beverly Havlir, & Delilah Devlin

NAUGHTY NIGHTS
by Charlene Teglia, Tawny Taylor, & Dawn Ryder

MIDNIGHT TREAT
by Sally Painter, Margaret L. Carter, & Shelley Munro

ROYAL BONDAGE
by Samantha Winston, Delilah Devlin, & Marianne LaCroix

MAGICAL SEDUCTION
by Cathryn Fox, Mandy M. Roth, & Anya Bast

GOOD GIRL SEEKS BAD RIDER
by Vonna Harper, Lena Matthews, & Ruth D. Kerce

ROAD TRIP TO PASSION
by Sahara Kelly, Lani Aames, & Vonna Harper

OVERTIME, UNDER HIM
by N.J. Walters, Susie Charles, & Jan Springer

GETTING WHAT SHE WANTS
by Diana Hunter, S.L. Carpenter, & Chris Tanglen

INSATIABLE
by Sherri L. King, Elizabeth Jewell, & S.L. Carpenter

HIS FANTASIES, HER DREAMS
by Sherri L. King, S.L. Carpenter, & Trista Ann Michaels

MASTER OF SECRET DESIRES
by S.L. Carpenter, Elizabeth Jewell, & Tawny Taylor

BEDTIME, PLAYTIME
by Jaid Black, Sherri L. King, & Ruth D. Kerce

HURTS SO GOOD
by Gail Faulkner, Lisa Renee Jones, & Sahara Kelly

LOVER FROM ANOTHER WORLD
by Rachel Carrington, Elizabeth Jewell, & Shiloh Walker

FEVER-HOT DREAMS
by Sherri L. King, Jaci Burton, & Samantha Winston

TAMING HIM
by Kimberly Dean, Summer Devon, & Michelle M. Pillow

ALL SHE WANTS
by Jaid Black, Dominique Adair, & Shiloh Walker

OUT OF THIS WORLD LOVER

SHANNON STACEY

SUMMER DEVON

CHARLENE TEGLIA

POCKET BOOKS

New York   London   Toronto   Sydney

Pocket Books
A Division of Simon & Schuster, Inc.
1230 Avenue of the Americas
New York, NY 10020

This book is a work of fiction. Names, characters, places, and incidents either are products of the authors' imagination, or are used fictitiously. Any resemblance to actual events or locales or persons, living or dead, is entirely coincidental.

Copyright © 2009 by Ellora's Cave Publishing, Inc.
Interstellar Sparks copyright © 2006 by Shannon Stacey
Futurelove copyright © 2006 by Summer Devon
Wolf in Cheap Clothing copyright © 2006 by Charlene Teglia

All rights reserved, including the right to reproduce
this book or portions thereof in any form whatsoever.
For information address Pocket Books Subsidiary Rights Department,
1230 Avenue of the Americas, New York, NY 10020

First Pocket Books trade paperback edition January 2009

POCKET and colophon are registered trademarks of Simon & Schuster, Inc.

For information about special discounts for bulk purchases,
please contact Simon & Schuster Special Sales
at 1-800-456-6798 or business@simonandschuster.com

Manufactured in the United States of America

10 9 8 7 6 5 4 3 2 1

Library of Congress Cataloging-in-Publication Data

Out of this world lover / Shannon Stacey, Summer Devon, Charlene Teglia. —
1st Pocket Books trade pbk. ed.
    p.   cm.   (Ellora's Cave anthologies)
 1. Erotic stories, American. I. Stacey Shannon. Interstellar sparks. II. Devon,
Summer. Futurelove. III. Teglia, Charlene. Wolf in cheap clothing.
  PS648.E7O83 2009
  813'.01083538—dc22   2008015434

ISBN-13: 978-1-4165-7825-3
ISBN-10:   1-4165-7825-0

CONTENTS

INTERSTELLAR SPARKS

SHANNON STACEY

ONE

New York City, 2144

ILYNA FOUND IT VERY difficult to focus on the borscht when what she really wanted served up was a toe-curling, back-arching, scream-inducing orgasm.

She daintily dabbed at her lips with her napkin and then smiled at the recently inaugurated American president. He blinked and smiled back. As the intergalactic ambassador from Acela, Ilyna was genetically engineered to be universally appealing to Earthlings. While the former president had been attracted to her keen intellect and political savvy, it was becoming increasingly clear the current president was most attracted to her breasts.

"How do you find your soup, Ambassador?" he asked politely, no doubt feeling the need to blandly converse after being caught so blatantly staring.

"It's perfect as always, Mr. President."

He nodded and they both returned to their meals. The epitome of grace and dignity. Not a soul in the room had any idea Ambassador Ilyna's thighs were pressed tightly together to keep her from squirming in her chair.

The scientist who'd manipulated her DNA must have had his

pocket protector out of whack the day he'd designed her sexuality. She was supposed to be perfect. She was beautiful, intelligent, politically adept, made sparkling conversation and never, ever succumbed to flatulence in public. Somehow she didn't imagine the Acelan scientists meant for their ambassador to be hiding intense and forbidden sexual desires behind her diplomat's mask.

Two hours later, Ilyna was squirming on the inside again. Why they insisted on throwing gala events in her honor was truly a mystery. The parties always included dancing—gorgeous women in gowns and jewels whirling around the room in the arms of handsome men in tuxedos. And one Acelan ambassador sitting in the corner with a plastic smile, beaming her approval. To her it seemed almost deliberately cruel.

The formal ballroom of the Windsor Interstellar Plaza Hotel was awash in glowing crystal, the shards of light reflecting off the women's jewelry. An unobtrusive orchestra sat behind a translucent veil, filling the room with notes of love and passion. She used to wonder if it was some devious plan to torture her, but over time she'd come to realize that the Earthlings included dancing in most of their formal events and never stopped to consider if it might be rude to include dancing in a party for a woman forbidden any physical contact with anyone not Acelan.

After a while, she wandered toward the tall windows overlooking a central courtyard. A few more minutes and she would say good night to the president and retire to her suite.

The lights were dimmed almost to darkness in the heavily vegetated courtyard so as not to distract from the glitter of the ballroom. The area was surrounded on all sides by the hotel, offering a haven only to those who could afford the exorbitant prices. A shadow shifted in the trees, and Ilyna stepped to the side of the window, peering into the near-darkness.

A man—a partygoer judging by the tuxedo—leaned against the post of a dimmed lamp, his head resting on the black metal. A brunette in a glittering designer gown knelt in front of him, the expensive fabric bunched carelessly around her thighs.

The man had his hand wound through the woman's hair, directing her head as it bobbed over his cock. One of her hands held her dress off the grass, the other cupped his balls, gently kneading. He lifted his head, smiling down at the woman as his grip on her head urged her on.

Ilyna pressed her palm to the window, surprised by the coolness of the glass against her own skin, which suddenly seemed feverishly hot. It surprised her that the couple would take such a risk, but perhaps the possibility of being watched excited them as much as watching them excited her.

Her breath caught in her throat then misted the glass when the man shifted, bending his knees slightly and bringing both hands to the back of the kneeling woman's head. He pulled her away for a moment, and Ilyna was given a glimpse of his glistening cock, moist with the woman's saliva. The woman's tongue flicked playfully over the head, and Ilyna's own tongue moistened her dry lips.

"Ambassador Ilyna!"

Startled, Ilyna spun away from the window to face Minister Jerrod's approach, her breath coming too rapidly. Not wanting him to see what she had stood witnessing through the glass, she moved quickly to meet him halfway.

The minister was short in stature and stout. His skin and hair were pale because the melanin meant to protect him from the planet's ultraviolet light was injected instead of built into his biological makeup as was hers. While she had, from conception, been intended for this diplomatic assignment, the ministers who accompanied her varied.

"I've been looking for you," he chastised, as though she'd done something wrong.

"I'm about to take my leave."

"Retiring so early, Ilyna?"

"Yes, Minister. I found the dancing wearying this evening."

Jerrod frowned, considering her words. "Wearying? I don't understand. You are not permitted contact with the people of Earth, so you couldn't possibly have danced."

No, but she could suffer the agony of having to watch. "The physical activity heated the room, and the temperature and the odors were tiring."

As was watching the men and women holding one another as they moved around the dance floor. Their bodies pressed together. Gazing into one another's eyes as their hands roamed their partners' backs, waists . . . and lower.

Ilyna hungered to feel a lover's touch. To feel his warm breath against her ear as he led her across the hardwood floor. She closed her eyes for the briefest of moments, imagining the feel of her partner's hair against her cheek. Imagined herself kneeling in the cool grass, taking her lover's cock deep into her mouth.

"You do look a little peaked," Jerrod said, and it took all of her self-control not to squirm under his appraising stare. "Go and rest now."

She would. Right after she plugged in her vibrator and her favorite digital partner. Orgasm first, then rest. "Good night, Minister."

THE ADHESIVE PATCH ITCHED like mad. As distractions went, it was minor, but it was chipping away at Ilyna's mood.

"Faster," she commanded. "Do it faster."

The blank expression on the face of the Greek god pumping into her didn't change. "I have achieved the maximum programmable rate of penetration."

"You are programmed to fulfill my every fantasy, and right now my fantasy is an increased rate of penetration."

"You are displeased. Shall I touch your breasts?"

Ilyna sighed and scratched at the adhesive patch over her nipple which fed a sensation of touch to her nerves. Ares wavered, a digital glitch flickering across his marble features. It was all so . . . false.

With a sigh, she withdrew the wired rubber phallus from her body. Then she pulled off the virtual sex visor and disentangled herself from the wires connecting the adhesive patches stuck on her erogenous zones. It wasn't enough anymore. And even if she had been allowed to mate, which she wasn't, that simply meant her virtual equipment would be integrated with her mate's virtual equipment. Acelans only exchanged bodily fluids by way of test tubes.

After cleaning and stowing the whole mess, she flopped back on the bed and stared at the big, dark video screen on the opposite wall. "Video on, volume low, channel three-nineteen."

One of the perks of the Ambassador Suite was complimentary, unmonitored access to every video feed, and it hadn't taken Ilyna long to discover the XXX station. She'd spent many hours watching the sexual interaction of humans on the big screen. Sometimes it wasn't very attractive, and quite often she had to mute the audio because of the bizarre mating noises, but she'd learned a lot about Earth sex.

Tonight's movie was billed as *Sparky and the Horny Housewife*, and Ilyna watched as the human woman called an electrician and then removed half her clothing. Within minutes of the man's arrival, the horny housewife was on her knees, sucking the stranger's cock even more enthusiastically than the woman she'd seen through the ballroom glass had her partner's.

Then the electrician bent her over the clear glass surface of the kitchen table. The camera beneath was treated to a mashed view of the horny housewife's nipples, and the squeaking of her flesh against the glass made Ilyna wince.

The view changed to a close-up of the electrician's cock sliding into the housewife's glistening pussy, before retreating and sliding home again. When she reached between her legs to squeeze his balls, the man groaned and quickened his pace.

"Fuck me faster. Do it faster," the horny housewife squealed. The man then pumped into her like a transport piston at high speed.

Ilyna sat straight up on the bed. That was it. She needed an electrician.

It took her ten minutes to figure out the telefile, but she couldn't very well buzz her aides and explain that she needed help playing horny housewife. The small black monitor next to the phone had a touch screen, and she finally wound her way through the menus to the electrical listings. Each name showed with credentials, contact info, and—thankfully—a photo.

She hadn't scrolled through many files before she found the face that stopped her in her tracks. He had short, tousled brown hair. Pretty baby blue eyes. A boyish grin, complete with dimples.

Bryan Cameron.

A rush of excitement made her fingers tremble as she wrote the contact information on a piece of hotel stationery. She scrolled through a few more files, and then blanked the screen. She had already found the electrician she was looking for.

Now came the hard part. Both incoming and outgoing transmissions were blocked on her room's unit. The only people she could reach were her companion, her head of security and Minister Jerrod himself. She would need Myscha's help.

Her companion answered immediately. "Yes, Ambassador?"

"Myscha, I want to go for a walk."

It was a plan they'd only executed three times before, but each time had been successful. She'd only gone for a walk those times, wanting to soak in the glass and steel of New York at her leisure. This time she'd be seeing to her pleasure. It was risky, true, but she would have no peace until this was done. She could do this without Minister Jerrod being any the wiser.

Myscha arrived several moments later dressed for a chilly autumn night. She wore a flowing woolen cloak that swirled around her, concealing her figure, which was leaner than Ilyna's. She had the hood up with a decorative scarf obscuring much of her face and carried a canvas shopping bag. Ten minutes later the bundled figure left the hotel in search of treats for the ambassador. Her desire for Earth chocolate was well-known.

Ilyna went a few blocks before stepping into a telephone kiosk. She took a deep breath, swiped her debit card and keyed in the number she'd written down. It rang several times before a male voice said, "Hello?"

"I need an electrician." Ilyna wanted to slap herself in the forehead. Where were her diplomatic skills now? It was customary to at least greet a person before making demands, even on the telephone.

"You found one, ma'am." His voice was low and rough, like maybe she'd woken him, and it made her already raw nerves sizzle. "What seems to be the problem?"

Problem? Oh, yes. The electrician in the video had been carrying tools. She scanned the telefile info she'd scribbled on the stationery, looking for any words that described what exactly he fixed.

"Wiring," she said. "I have a wiring problem."

He didn't laugh, but he made a little snorting sound that made her sure he wanted to. "Why don't you give me your location, and I'll swing by and give you an estimate in the morning?"

"In the morning? It's . . . rather more urgent than that, I'm afraid. I'm at the Windsor Interstellar Plaza Hotel. The Ambassador Suite, floor 139."

"Wow." He was quiet for so long she feared they'd lost transmission. "If you're having electrical problems in a five-star interstellar hotel suite, you buzz the concierge. That's his job."

"Oh." She didn't see that coming. But spontaneous prevarication was second nature to a diplomat. "I'd rather the concierge not be aware of this problem. I caused it, you see."

"Ma'am, that's not something—"

"Am I interrupting your family? Will your wife be upset if you work?"

"No, I live alone, ma'am, but I can't just walk into the Windsor and start tinkering with their wiring. If you can afford the Ambassador Suite, you can afford to compensate them for any damages to it. Good luck."

A beep indicated he'd disconnected, and Ilyna frowned at the handset. There was no way she was letting him off that easily. She wasn't going back to her room until she'd experienced some real Earth sex.

BRYAN CAMERON HAD SHAKEN off the weird call from the rich lady, taken a leak and was ignoring a customer bid he needed to write up in favor of watching a game when his doorbell chimed.

A glance at his watch confirmed that it was as late as he thought it was, and concern for his brother rippled through him. But he opened the door to find a tall, blonde, almost unrealistically gorgeous woman standing there staring at him. Her pale skin was accented by full, rosy lips and brilliant green eyes ringed by smoky, thick eyelashes. And her body . . . he just tried not to stare.

"Are you Bryan Cameron? The electrician?"

Her voice was as sexy as her body and his dick twitched as if her words had reached down and stroked him. "Yeah. What can I do for you?"

"I'm Ilyna . . . from the Windsor."

She stopped talking, and Bryan got the impression she had no idea what to say next. "Why, exactly, did you even call me earlier? Better yet, why did you come to my house?"

She blinked, and then gave him a shy smile. "Because electricians do it faster. I saw that in a pornographic movie and decided to find an electrician."

Whoa. Faster? "Is that . . . a good thing or a bad thing?"

"It's a good thing. If I say *faster*, you will increase your rate of penetration."

"Geez, lady, you sound like Mrs. Farroway."

"Did Mrs. Farroway like fast penetration as well?"

His balls tried to climb up to safety at the thought. "No, she was my tenth-grade Language Sciences teacher. And the most unattractive woman on the planet."

The woman took a deep breath. "I want to have sex with you."

That was certainly blunt enough. He tried to come up with an intelligent response to what seemed like the best luck he'd ever been struck by, but all he could say was, "Why?"

The woman stepped closer. "Does it matter? I know I'm beautiful, and you told me you live alone. Don't men like . . . what are they? One-night stands?"

This was some kind of practical joke. It had to be. "What's your name, sweetheart?"

"Ilyna."

Ilyna. The name seemed familiar somehow, but he couldn't place it. Meanwhile he could well imagine the bad angel jumping from one shoulder to the other to beat the crap out of his good angel.

"Did Dane send you?"

"No," she said quickly, and then she made a face and a hand gesture that reminded him of a person recognizing an opportunity had just slipped by.

She walked slowly forward, until she was well within arm's reach. "I just want to have sex with you. After that I want nothing else from you, and you'll never see me again."

She reached out and popped the snap on his jeans. Bryan groaned. Some practical joke. The guys would never let him live this down. His cock didn't seem to care—it strained against his zipper.

"Lady, I don't think . . ."

She slipped the heavy robe from her shoulders, stepped out of a silky-looking gown, and he forgot to think at all.

TWO

EVERY MAN'S FANTASY WAS standing right in front of him—oh geez, *kneeling* right in front of him—and Bryan was at a total loss. A sigh of relief escaped him when she slid his zipper down and then eased his jeans and boxers down over his hips, baring his throbbing erection.

"What," he asked through gritted teeth, "are you doing?"

"I want to suck you," she said simply, and his knees almost buckled. What the hell was going on?

"Usually I know a woman a little better before the blow jobs start, sweetheart."

She smiled, an act that lit up her face like a beacon. "I'm Ilyna. You're Bryan."

And then she touched her lips to the tip of his cock and Bryan's knees almost gave out. The warmth of her mouth closed over him, sucking gently, and he groaned. His hips twitched, and he felt her smile around his cock. Fuck it—who was he to deny a beautiful woman a one-night stand?

Threading his fingers in Ilyna's hair, he tugged gently, pushing deeper into her mouth, then retreating. She made a humming sound low in her throat and his balls tightened. She pulled back and licked delicately at the now wet head of his cock. The slight, kittenish strokes of her tongue almost put him over the edge and he pulled away. "You've got one more chance to walk out that door before I give in and fuck you."

She looked up at him through those thick eyelashes and licked her lips. "I want to suck you some more."

"If you suck me anymore, I think you'll kill me." Her eyes widened in alarm, and he chuckled. "It's just an expression. But it's your turn now, sweetheart."

ILYNA GASPED WHEN BRYAN sat her on the edge of the bed and then knelt on the lavishly plush carpet. "I want to taste you," he said.

Ilyna shuddered in anticipation. "Taste me?"

He only smiled and lifted her legs to hook her knees over his shoulders. She craned her neck to see better.

His mouth was hot and moist on her pussy. With a moan she fell back to her elbows, letting her head drop back.

His tongue slid into her, thrusting, before withdrawing to circle lazily around her clit. Ilyna balled the bedspread in her fists and tried not to scream in pleasure. Every single nerve ending in her body was centered on that small nub. Her flesh tingled, and an ache at the small of her back demanded release.

Bryan covered her pussy with his mouth and sucked. First gently, then with more pressure. She let go of the blanket and pushed her fingers into his hair, trying to press his mouth against her.

Bryan lifted his face to look at her. "Like that, sweetheart?"

She tried to speak, then gave up and simply nodded. He feasted on her body like a starving man, and soon Ilyna couldn't even think. She could only arch her back and moan as the orgasm took her like she'd never been taken before.

Bryan made her come twice before he grasped her wrists and pulled her to a sitting position. He kissed her, and Ilyna tasted her own juices on his lips. His tongue slid over hers and he nipped not-so-gently at her bottom lip.

He tucked his arms under her knees and drew her to the edge of the bed, exposing her glistening pussy. She felt vulnerable, but his gaze was hot and she didn't feel any shame.

When the thick head of his cock finally breached her soft opening, Ilyna almost wept for joy. His erection was as hard and filling as she'd expected, but the heat was a pleasant surprise. For the first time in her life, she was being fucked by a live man, and she knew then she'd ruined herself. Rubber just wasn't going to cut it anymore.

He held back as she stretched to accommodate him, but soon his cock was buried to the hilt, and Ilyna rocked her pelvis. His balls slapped against her ass and she moaned.

"Oh yes," she whispered.

Bryan pulled out—all the way—and then plunged back into her. She came again, her fingernails raking the backs of her own thighs as he pinned her legs to his chest with strong arms. Her hips bucked and she thrashed her head as the muscles in her body spasmed with pleasure.

She'd barely caught her breath when Bryan slipped out of her body and rolled her over. With her feet on the floor she bent over the bed, still panting.

"I don't know what I did to deserve you," he said, easing his dick back into her pussy, "but you are beautiful as hell when you come, sweetheart."

With this new angle, Ilyna felt the pressure of his erection even deeper—a feeling that bordered on pain, until the pleasure obliterated it. He pressed down on the small of her back with one hand, while the other reached between her legs to massage her clit. She sobbed, feeling the intensity of her impending orgasm build. Instinctively she reached back with her right hand and cupped his balls, rolling the taut sac in her hand.

"Fuck me . . . faster," Ilyna moaned, and Bryan complied, pounding into her until she let go of his scrotum and once again balled the bedspread in her fists.

His fingers left her clit and he grabbed hold of her hips with both hands, pumping his cock into her faster and faster until she screamed into the mattress, her body quaking with the release. Bryan shouted, a low, guttural sound, and his movements slowed, became erratic as he poured himself into her.

When she had caught her breath and could speak again, Ilyna said, "That was incredible. I never dreamed it could be like that."

Bryan flopped down on the mattress and pulled her up against his side. "That *was* incredible. Give me a few minutes and we'll do it again."

Ilyna smiled. Who knew electricians could be so handy?

BRYAN JERKED AWAKE WHEN the warm, soft body next to him suddenly scrambled out of bed as if the blankets were on fire. He blinked, watching her pace in panicked circles until she stopped, throwing her hands up in the air.

"I didn't mean to fall asleep," she said, sounding on the verge of tears.

Oh shit, she's married, he thought, ignoring the unexpected pang of regret that caused. "It's pretty common after multiple orgasms, sweetheart."

"Why didn't you tell me that?" Her voice trembled and Bryan wondered exactly how angry somebody was going to be that Ilyna wasn't in her room. He wasn't going to let anybody put their hands on her in anger.

"I didn't know you had a curfew. It's still early. Maybe you can tiptoe in without being seen."

She shook her head, staring down at the carpet. "I was supposed to meet Minister Jerrod at six this morning to prepare for our breakfast with the president."

"The president? President Fletcher?" Bryan's mind blanked for a second, and then the pieces fell into place. "Jerrod . . . oh shit. You're the freakin' ambassador from that planet."

"Acela."

Bryan sat on the bed next to her and put his head in his hands. "This is bad."

"Yes, it is."

"We're not even supposed to shake hands with you, never mind bend you over the damn bed."

"No, you're not. Although I did enjoy that very much, and if more people did that, there would be much less conflict in the universe."

"There has to be some way to keep people from knowing."

Ilyna shook her head again, a slow, mournful movement. "Minister Jerrod already knows I was out during the night. He'll screen me and know that I've been contaminated."

"Contaminated?" Bryan stood and started pacing. "Contaminated by me?"

"No!" She stood and threw herself into his arms, and he couldn't help wrapping them around her and pulling her close. She was shaking so hard he was surprised her teeth weren't rattling. "I didn't mean that, Bryan. It's just a phrase our scientists use. When you live in an artificial habitat you're very careful about the foreign particles and germs you allow in."

He pressed a kiss to her hair. "What will they do to you if they find out? They won't kill you, will they? Stone you to death in the town square or something?"

"That would be barbaric."

"Okay. So what are the consequences for fucking a guy from the wrong side of the portal?"

"They will mutilate my face and genitalia to prevent further transgressions. Then I will serve in some domestic capacity."

"*What?*" Bryan's gut twisted at the idea of some bastard mutilating any part of her beautiful body. "And that's not barbaric?"

"Is it not better to live as an ugly slave than to be dead?"

"I don't know. Why the hell would you do it, Ilyna? Why would you sneak out and come to me, knowing the consequences?"

"Because of the modifications done to my genetic material, I am forbidden to mate, to procreate."

"Forbidden to mate? You mean like . . . ever?"

"On Acela, only wedded mates may have sexual relations—digitally, of course. As ambassador, I'm forbidden to wed. Although, since you and I have had sexual relations, that makes you my husband."

He almost choked on his tongue. How the hell had he gone from a one-night stand with a beautiful woman to having a renegade alien ambassador for a wife? Forget the guys never letting him live this down. They were never going to believe him in the first place.

"I was destined to find my pleasure with plastic and wires and digital partners." She grasped his hand, pressing her palm to his. "But with you, I'm truly alive. Your body generates this incredible heat and warms my own. Your breath is so warm, but when you blow across my damp flesh it's cool. I love the roughness of your hands and the smooth silkiness of your tongue. I love the feel of you. Your scent. Your taste."

"My taste is not worth your being a slave, sweetheart."

"I was already a slave, Bryan. My body has belonged to them since my conception. I have no freedom. Only the illusion of it."

He stood for a moment, simply holding her and considering the situation. She wasn't simply a missing person. She was a creation in which the Acelan government had no doubt invested a great deal of time and money. They weren't going to simply shrug their collective shoulders and head back to their home planet to grow themselves another ambassador. And if it meant averting an intergalactic crisis, his own government wouldn't be shrugging their own collective shoulders, either.

"They're going to connect you to me, Ilyna. And when they do they'll probably arrive with a substantial amount of muscle and firepower."

"How can they know I'm with you?"

"Did you call from your suite?"

A victorious smile lit up her face. "No. I called from a public booth. You see?"

"How did you get my number?"

"From the electronic telefile in . . . " She paused, the light fading from her eyes. "It was in my suite. Will it remember which files I called for?"

Bryan nodded, feeling sick to his stomach. He barely spared a thought to whether or not there would be consequences for him. It was just unfathomable to him that this sweet, gorgeous woman had to risk her well-being to get the physical affection she had so obviously been starving for.

"Oh, and I used my debit card. How could I be so stupid? They will definitely find us here. I'd never considered running away, but . . . why not? Do you know anybody who could take us in? Friends? Family?"

"No."

She arched one of those exquisite brows at him and he knew she didn't believe him. "Okay, I have one brother. His name is Dane. He's four years older, and we're not going to him."

"Oh. Okay."

Bryan had enough experience with women to know what kind of thoughts were flying around behind those puppy-dog eyes. Thoughts about her not being good enough to meet his family. About his being embarrassed by her. Or that she wasn't important enough to merit putting his brother at risk.

"Look," he said softly, trying to get his brain to consider his words before his mouth engaged. "Dane isn't a very nice guy. And I don't think an . . . adult entertainment complex is a good place to take you."

That got her attention. "A sex club? Your brother owns a real licensed sex club?"

"Forget it." Bryan scrubbed his face with his hands, wishing he could simply wipe the mention of Dane from her memory. "What the hell do you know about sex clubs, anyway?"

"I know that in 2119 your government realized that prostitution, underage slavery, sexually transmitted diseases and sex crimes were escalating to epidemic proportions. After eight years of studies and debates, they legalized the ownership of licensed and strictly regulated adult entertainment complexes. The first five years of operation saw an almost *seventy* percent drop in those same problem areas. From then on, the sex clubs have been not only legal, but encouraged and mainstreamed."

Bryan held up a hand to stem her little history lesson. "It was a rhetorical question, sweetheart."

Her face was awash with enthusiasm for her subject. Why the hell hadn't she landed on Dane's doorstep? His horny resident alien and his jaded older brother would no doubt be a perfect match.

An ancient, acute case of sibling envy punched him in the gut. Dane *always* got the girls. He had the best wheels, the hottest babes and the most insanely jealous little brother on the planet.

But Dane wasn't an electrician and because of some stupid porn video, that's what Ilyna had gone looking for. Lucky Bryan.

"You look angry," she said quietly. "But it would be an excellent temporary solution to our situation. They would never believe I would take refuge in a place like that. And the clubs have so many safeguards for their patrons' privacy."

It was a losing battle, but he couldn't sound the retreat quite yet. The idea of setting Ilyna loose in a place like *Ris*-K made his palms sweat. And not in a good way. "If you're in trouble for having sex with a human, the solution is not to go hang out in a sex club full of them. And I don't know if this has occurred to you, but you've brought me into this situation. Now you're asking me to drag my brother into aiding and abetting in the hiding of an intergalactic ambassador to Earth."

Her mouth made a little O, and then her face changed. Ilyna's back straightened and her chin lifted. A polite half smile curved her lips as she stepped away from him. "Of course. How selfish of me. If you would be so kind as to dial the hotel, I will have Minister Jerrod send a car for me."

Bryan blinked at the woman before him. Gone was his horny little alien. There was no trace of the woman who'd screamed his name into his pillow last night. Now here, even with bedhead and her life in shambles, was Ambassador Ilyna—a woman known the universe over for her ability to negotiate with the most powerful men in the galaxy, to bring even the most fierce warrior planets to use the proper fork at the president's table.

It broke his heart. No woman should have a life that enabled her to instantly and thoroughly be somebody she wasn't. "I'll call Dane. Since we're up to no good, he'll probably welcome us with open arms. He gets off on this kind of shit."

A SLEEK, BLACK LUXURY hydrocar purred to a stop in front of Bryan's house an hour later, and Ilyna suppressed a shiver of excitement. Yesterday she'd despaired for her future, and now today Bryan Cameron was taking her to *Ris*-K—a real, live Earth sex club.

She was peeking through the blinds when a man got out of the passenger side of the car and walked with long, unhurried strides toward the house. He looked a little like Bryan, but he was darker and rougher and maybe just a little dangerous. She jumped back when he looked straight at her, but he'd made eye contact.

Ilyna heard the front door open and the low murmur of voices before both men appeared in the kitchen. Dane approached her slowly, but stopped about two feet in front of her. With his hands behind his back, he bowed slightly from the waist. It was the customary greeting for an Acelan delegate, and Ilyna nodded her head in response.

"Ambassador, I'm Dane Cameron. I understand you'll be my guest for the immediate future."

"It's a pleasure."

A naughty smile jerked up the corners of his mouth. "You have no idea how much of a pleasure it will be."

Bryan cleared his throat and in the next moment he was at her side. She stepped into his hold, feeling an unfamiliar thrill at the possessive gesture. "I'm going to lock her in our suite until she's old and ugly."

That was less thrilling. She gave him her best power look. "I may as well return to Acela if I am to be kept locked up until I'm an old woman."

Both men laughed, and she recognized too late the human tendency toward wild exaggeration as humor. Most of the Earthlings she'd spoken with had no discernable senses of humor. "That is *not* funny, Bryan."

"We should go," Dane said abruptly, bringing their attention back to the matter at hand. "Is everything ready?"

Bryan nodded and Dane stepped away to speak into a tiny comm unit. Mere seconds later, Bryan's work hydrovan backed down the driveway and took off up the street. Another man entered the foyer and took the bags Bryan had packed and left there. They followed him out and were soon settled in the backseat, while Dane rode up front with his driver. Before he'd closed the door, however, he'd dropped a packet of paper in Ilyna's lap. Once they were under way, she gave it her full attention.

"What is all this?" She riffled through the pages, trying to make some sense of the barrage of legalese. Her IQ was extremely high in Earth terms, but legal documentation was usually handled by Minister Jerrod.

"The cost of entertainment," Bryan muttered. "Dane's willing to take us in knowing we're fugitives, but it's in everybody's best interest if the formalities are taken care of. It might help protect him if things go badly."

He began explaining the forms to her and pointing out where she needed to sign. There were forms demanding disclosure of her sexual health and any criminal records to be confirmed by their blood scans and databases. There was a form releasing *Ris*-K and

Dane Cameron from liability for everything from paper cuts up to and including a nuclear detonation.

"What is this one for?"

Bryan scanned the paper. "You have to acknowledge that all areas of the club are under video surveillance. It means everything's being taped. All video feeds are kept for one year, and then deleted."

She frowned. "I thought privacy was of utmost importance at sex clubs."

"It is. If Dane was caught showing those feeds around he would lose everything and go to prison to boot. They're only viewed if you're accused of a violent crime within *Ris-K*, and even then they can only be released to the senior officer in charge of the investigation. It's for the protection of his guests, and Dane takes his responsibilities to them very seriously."

"Why don't *you* have to fill out all these forms?" she asked. She was growing weary of the bureaucratic red tape. She wanted to see the club.

"I'm there all the time. I have to go through health scanning each time, but I can skip the red tape."

"All the time?" Ilyna wasn't sure she liked the sound of that. "Doing what?"

"Well, it ain't a bridge club, sweetheart," he said in a suggestive voice, and then he winked at her.

"You have sex with women *all the time?*" For the first time in her twenty-eight Earth years of life, Ilyna lost her temper. She whacked him in the shoulder with the clipboard.

He laughed at her. "No, I don't. But I try to visit Dane regularly, and to see him, I have to go to the club. To get in, I had to do the forms."

"But you have sex with women sometimes." He had to in order

to be so wondrously good at it. She just hoped he wouldn't have sex with other women during this visit.

"I'm no ambassador, but this calls for an abrupt change of subject," he said, dodging when she tried to hit him again. "So you have no sunlight on Acela?"

She thought about it, then decided to go along with the change. If they kept on in the current vein, she might get answers she'd rather not hear. "We have some, but it's extremely weak compared to yours. We rely on artificial lighting and heating."

"So how can you be outside when you're on Earth? Your skin must burn like a newborn baby's."

"Melanin is engineered into my cell structure. Don't forget, I was designed specifically for Earth. Myscha was also designed for Earth, as her purpose was always to serve me. But—"

"Wait. They genetically engineered you a servant?"

"She's my companion. We've been together since childhood. We are so well-bonded I don't even have to speak my needs as a rule. She's excellent in her position."

"And Jerrod?"

Ilyna grimaced. "The minister is a high-ranking member of the Acelan government, and I'm not always accompanied by the same minister. Jerrod does request Earth service a great deal, but he wasn't genetically intended for it, so his melanin is injected. That's why he is so pale and must use extreme caution when he leaves the hotel. He is also treated with . . . something like steroids to enable him to breathe your atmosphere."

"I don't understand how you come to be from a planet that requires artificial light and heat to be inhabitable."

"Long before I was born—"

"Hatched?"

"*Born*, a group of scientists launched an experiment to see if a colony could be established on a distant planet. The planet didn't have an ideal atmosphere, so an artificial habitat was needed. The experiment—Acela—grew and grew, until several hundred of the home planet's finest minds were in the habitat, which over the course of fifty years or so had grown to be nearly self-sufficient.

"But in the confined, artificial environment, contamination from the home planet was a constant danger. In the sixty-first year of the experiment, Acela declared its independence. The home planet fought back, and I understand things were very tense in the habitat. Then the home planet sent a delegation and it was obvious that they couldn't come to terms. Three weeks later the home planet was dead."

"What do you mean the planet was dead?"

"Every living thing on the planet was no longer living."

"Within three weeks of pissing off several hundred of the finest scientific minds in the galaxy? What a coincidence."

"Yes. And you pretty much know the rest. Genetic engineering, scientific superiority, extreme measures against contamination."

He leaned close to her, his breath hot on her cheek, his fingers sliding up under her short dress. "I like contaminating you."

Ilyna spread her thighs as her body welcomed his touch with warm moisture. His fingers brushed her clit and her hips bucked against his hand. "Are you going to contaminate me now?"

Bryan chuckled into her hair. "With my brother and his driver in the front seat? They could drop that privacy glass anytime, you know."

She looked at the blackened glass, her breath shortening. They could be discreet. After all, his hand was hidden by her skirt. "Then contaminate me fast."

"Pull your skirt up around your waist." She wasn't wearing

any panties, and the cool, climate-controlled air made her shiver. "Knees apart."

She paused, glancing at the privacy glass. He pulled away from her, punishing her hesitation with the absence of his touch.

"Do it now, Ilyna."

She spread her knees, opening herself to him and risking exposing herself to Dane if he lowered the screen. The vulnerability bothered her until Bryan touched a finger to her lips. She drew it into her mouth, sucking it as enthusiastically as she'd sucked his cock the night before. She flicked her tongue over the calluses, loving the feel of his work-roughened hands.

Bryan withdrew his finger from her mouth and inserted it slowly into her pussy, his eyes never leaving her face. He twisted his finger, his knuckle rubbing against her inner walls in all the right places. She leaned her head back, closing her eyes.

"Don't," he demanded in a harsh whisper. "I want you to watch my fingers fucking you."

A spasm of pleasure shuddered through her body as Bryan slipped another finger into her cunt. She watched them sliding in and out of her body, glistening with her juices. Her hips rocked up to meet his thrust of his hand, and she was hopeless to stop the small whimpering sounds coming from her throat.

Ilyna reached down and circled her clit with her own finger, loving the way her hand bumped against Bryan's. He eased a third finger into her, and the delicious stretching of her pussy to fit them had her teetering on the brink.

Then he slid his fingers out of her and she moaned in protest. She was so close to coming, and this was just cruel.

"Fuck yourself," he whispered. "Fuck yourself with your fingers so I can watch."

Obediently she slid her middle finger down through her folds and pressed it into her pussy. With her thumb she continued lightly rubbing her clit, and the sensation—along with the delicious naughtiness of knowing she could be caught by Dane Cameron at any second while Bryan looked on—returned her to the brink of orgasm.

"Another finger," Bryan demanded, and she moaned as a second finger joined the first. "Don't come yet."

"Please," she whimpered.

"Not yet." His finger ran over hers, sliding in the juices, pressing down on her hand for a moment, before continuing on. The wet tip of his finger traced the crack of her ass, then settled against the small, puckered hole. "Fuck yourself faster, sweetheart."

Ilyna looked down, watching her fingers sliding in and out of her pussy and her thumb pressing on her clit. She saw and felt Bryan's finger enter behind her own and her back arched on the leather seat.

Through the mind-blowing haze of her orgasm, she heard Bryan growl, "You are so fucking hot when you come."

Finally the tremors passed, and she was vaguely aware of Bryan pulling her skirt down.

"The car stopped, sweetheart." He lifted her hand and sucked her juices from her fingers. "We're here."

She was still panting when the back door swung open and a uniformed man said, "Welcome to *Ris*-K."

THREE

ILYNA'S DISAPPOINTMENT UPON ARRIVING at *Ris*-K was keen and she made it known.

"Why can't I look around now?" She tried to inject a pleading note into her voice, but she herself could hear the imperious tone. She was accustomed to humans being slightly more solicitous when dealing with her wants and needs.

"Ambassador," Dane responded evenly, "I would like to see you settled in your suite first so I have time to brief my key personnel on this situation. I'm sure you wouldn't wish to satisfy your curiosity at the expense of *Ris*-K."

The censure was so smoothly delivered Ilyna thought he would make an excellent diplomat should he ever give up the sex business.

They'd passed through several large anterooms in which she'd handed over her paperwork and been subjected to blood tests and a full body scan. Now she was being hustled through a massive dining area, and she tried to walk slower so as to buy more time to look around.

The décor was much more elegant than she'd anticipated. The rich cream walls and black lacquered wood set off the jewel tones used through the room. It all looked very tasteful for a sex club, in her opinion. Even the bare-breasted women serving the dishes looked as though they'd be right at home at the Windsor Interstellar Plaza Hotel.

They rushed her much too quickly through a lounge featuring a stage on which a woman appeared to be showering in a glass box. The crowd seemed very appreciative of her self-lathering.

"Most of the sex takes place in assigned areas and private rooms," Dane whispered in her ear.

"Oh. So I won't get to see?"

He laughed and slapped Bryan between the shoulder blades. "You got yourself a kinky one this time, brother."

He ushered them into a private elevator before saying, "There are observation mirrors for the safety of our guests. Normally it's forbidden, but I might be able to turn my back for a few minutes if my brother decides to give you a tour."

"Won't you get in trouble?"

"Only if you tell. And you'll be the first person I've ever permitted in the hallways. A special perk for being my brother's girl."

The brother in question was standing right behind her, and she could feel his erection against the curve of her hip. Hearing herself referred to as Bryan's girl made her want nothing more than to be alone with him. "I think we'll enjoy our suite for a while first, but I'm sure we'll avail ourselves of your generous offer soon."

The elevator door slid open and they stepped into a long hallway. The décor of the dining room seemed to continue through the rest of the club and Ilyna found herself impressed by the atmosphere Dane had built. There was nothing sleazy or cheap about *Ris*-K.

He led them to Suite 35 and swiped the key card before hand-ing it to Bryan. "Enjoy. And call the concierge for anything you need."

Bryan nodded and pushed Ilyna through the door, slamming it behind him. She barely had time to register what looked like a really nice suite before he tossed her onto the sapphire-hued leather couch.

"Do it again."

She didn't even need to ask what he meant. With him looming over her, she slowly lifted her skirt. Then, after swirling her finger around in her mouth until he groaned with impatience, she slid it into her pussy. She didn't watch herself this time, but watched him watching her. Just to tease him she removed her finger and sucked it again before sliding two fingers back into her cunt.

"You're so beautiful, Ilyna. I could watch you fuck yourself forever."

"It's not the same," she whispered. "Nothing feels as good as your cock sliding into me."

"Soon, babe. Right now I want to watch you make yourself come."

Bryan undid his jeans, lowering them on his hips just enough to free his cock. He gripped it in his hand, squeezing its length from the base to the tip. Ilyna watched him stroke himself and easily slid a third finger into her now dripping pussy.

His eyes never wavered from her probing fingers as he jerked himself off, his left hand dropping to cup his balls. He was rougher with himself than she was, squeezing his dick harder than she dared. Her body quickened as she neared orgasm and she became mesmerized by the sight of the small drop glistening at the tip of his cock. Ilyna licked her lips, eager to suck it for him, but he didn't even notice. His strokes quickened and the devouring look on his face sent her over the edge. She lifted her hips, forcing her fingers deeper into her pussy as she came, feeling the walls squeeze and tense around her knuckles.

Bryan released his cock and grabbed Ilyna's hand. He sucked her juices from her fingers, swirling his tongue around each finger until she squirmed. Then he rolled her to her knees on the couch. She shifted to bend over the arm, and Bryan entered her from behind in one swift, hard motion. Her breath caught in her throat as he pounded into her, his balls slapping against her clit.

"You're a naughty girl," he said through gritted teeth. Then he slapped her ass and the sting made her gasp. She rocked back hard against him, meeting his thrusts as he spanked her again. "But you're only naughty with me. Do you understand?"

She couldn't speak—every muscle and nerve in her body was focused on his cock driving into her.

He grasped her hair, pulling her head up. "Only me, Ilyna. Say it."

"Only you, Bryan," she whispered, her voice choked as she came, driving herself backward again and again, impaling herself on Bryan's cock. They came together, and then he buried his face in her hair.

"Don't forget," he whispered.

BRYAN ENTERED THEIR SUITE with a sigh of relief. With that wiring job out of the way, he could now be officially on vacation for a while.

A short while. The thought he'd been trying to bury all day resurfaced again, and it was persistent this time. He couldn't live with Ilyna at *Ris*-K forever.

Well, technically it was possible, but for two problems. One, he didn't want to live at *Ris*-K. It was his brother's world, and as far different from his dreams as his brother was from him. And two, the Acelans were no doubt stepping up the heat on the government even now. Eventually they would have to leave or Dane could lose everything.

And, while she hadn't been in his life very long, Bryan couldn't leave her behind. He couldn't go back to his normal, safe—lonely—life without her. She'd gotten under his skin, and he'd surprised himself by deciding he'd give it all up for this woman he barely knew.

Ilyna appeared from the kitchen. She beamed at him, and he opened his arms for a hug. She grabbed his crotch instead.

"Come and give me some of that, big daddy."

He winced and backed away a couple of steps. "What did you say?"

Ilyna leaned forward and pressed her breasts together. "Come and get it, big daddy."

"That's, uh . . . kinda creepy, sweetheart."

Her face fell, the sexy pout fading into a plain old pout, and he regretted his words instantly.

"Creepy?" she asked uncertainly. "Is my slang wrong, because I was trying to make you feel horny, not repulsed."

"I'm not repulsed. Really. I just . . . how about you watch a different channel for a while? We need to find you some shows that aren't all about sex."

She was quiet, pensive, and then her face brightened. "Good evening, husband. I hope you had a pleasant day today."

The flat, almost robotic tone she used freaked Bryan out even more than her use of the word *husband*.

"It was fine," he said warily, dropping his key cards and loose change on a side table.

"Please sit while I prepare your favorite foods. When a man

works hard all day, he deserves nothing but the finest treatment at home."

Bryan wished her smile didn't look quite so fake. He slid into his chair, never taking his eyes off her. Maybe this was some weird Acelan PMS thing. He had to admit, life with Ilyna was never boring.

"I tired of the sex channel and watched an old movie about perfect wives," she explained. "I think they may have been robots, but their husbands seemed pleased."

He laughed then, and shook his head. "Promise me you'll never watch the murder mystery channel, okay?"

"I promise . . . if you bring me on the tour of *Ris*-K your brother mentioned."

Bryan took a deep breath, but he knew he couldn't put it off anymore. He was afraid if he didn't take her around the club him-self, she'd sneak out of their suite and God only knew what trouble she'd get into on her own.

"We'll go down for dinner and see where it goes from there, okay?"

When Ilyna squealed and ran into the bedroom, he couldn't help but chuckle at her enthusiasm. Only a few moments later she emerged in a barely there white sheath. He whistled his ap-preciation, making a mental note to thank Dane for the clothes he'd provided for Ilyna, and put out his arm for her to take. She lifted her chin and nodded her thanks, looking every inch the ambassador. Except, of course, for her bare hand touching his forearm.

They had no reservation for the dining room—*Ris*-K had a reputation not only for sex but for having one of the best chefs in the city—but they were seated at the table usually reserved for Dane's use. Formal dining was an activity in which Ilyna was not only skilled, but comfortable, and soon they were enjoying the finest of wines and each other's company.

The sexual tension in the room was high—the diners had either just lived out their sexual fantasies or were anticipating doing so after their meals. But Bryan was relieved she seemed content to focus on him. They talked a little about his childhood. Bryan and Dane had gone into foster care early in their lives and had remained there until their foster father disappeared when he was a teenager. Dane had been old enough to care for him then, and it all remained an overall unremarkable time of his life. Then the subject switched to his work and he tried to think of stories that would make her laugh. It was a rich, beautiful sound that turned the head of every man in the room.

She leaned in close across the table. "Did you ever have a horny housewife call you to go have sex with her?"

Bryan laughed and shook his head. "No, but I think I saw that movie at the electrical inspector's bachelor party. I did have a horny alien ambassador show up at my door, though, wanting to use my body for sex."

Her face softened and a hint of pink tinted her pale cheeks. "Did you let her?"

"I did. I didn't even charge her for it. Electricians aren't known for freebies, either."

"Were you sorry you let her in?"

"No, sweetheart. It was the best job I ever landed."

She looked as though she might cry—something he wasn't even sure she had the capacity for—and Bryan was relieved when their server appeared to ask if they wanted dessert.

"No thank you," Ilyna answered. "I brought my own."

Bryan felt as confused as the server looked, but he passed also and she went on to the next table. "You brought your own?"

She leaned forward, a playful smile tugging at the corners of her mouth. "I want to suck your cock until you come in my mouth."

He almost snapped the stem of his wineglass in two. "Umm . . . well, that's direct."

Bryan was talking to air. Ilyna had already slipped under the long drape of the tablecloth. He thought about dragging her out and taking her back to the suite, but what the hell? He undid his jeans and worked his cock free. It was already hard and it jumped in his hand when Ilyna's soft, warm lips pressed a kiss against the tip. He let her take over then and tried to keep his hand nonchalantly on the table.

She drew him in slowly, and not being able to see her was excruciating. He had to force himself not to fling the table away so he could see his dick sliding in between her rosy lips. His sac tightened and he almost groaned aloud. This wasn't going to take very long.

His hips tried to rock in his chair as Ilyna's mouth traveled up and down his erection, pausing now and again so she could run her tongue over the tiny slit in the head before taking him deep against her throat again. Dishes rattled and he forced himself to ease his grip on the tablecloth.

When her fist joined in the gentle strokes, he threw back his head and closed his eyes, audience be damned. Lubricated by her saliva, her fist squeezed a path behind her mouth. First up, then down, until he couldn't stand it anymore. When her other hand began caressing his balls, while the double whammy of her hand and mouth still worked his dick, he came. He reached down with one hand, holding the back of her head as she drank him in, her mouth still milking the come from his throbbing cock.

Then she reappeared and sat in her chair as if nothing was amiss. Taking the white linen napkin from the edge of the table, she daintily wiped the corners of her mouth and smiled. "I'm ready for my tour now."

Bryan pressed a hand to his racing heart. "I'm going to need a moment, sweetheart."

ILYNA COULDN'T BELIEVE THE number of ways humans found to have sex with one another. Dressed in matching, emerald satin *Ris*-K robes, they explored the hidden hallways that were restricted to Dane and his head of security. Each room had a two-way mirror so Bryan and Ilyna could see the activities going on inside, though they could hear nothing. Every room in the club had maximum soundproofing.

She'd seen whips, feathers, whipped cream and a small group of men happily screwing watermelons and cantaloupes on a red-and-white checked picnic cloth. They'd sped by most of the fetish areas, although Ilyna had been momentarily fascinated by a man jerking off into a red leather boot. She'd also enjoyed watching the "Viking" pillaging and plundering once Bryan assured her the women worked for Dane and were paid very well to be willingly pillaged and plundered.

They paused at the next window and Ilyna marveled at the tangle of arms and legs. How did somebody not have an eye poked out?

She watched silently for a moment, trying to count how many bodies writhed in the pile. Something was missing.

"Bryan, there is no man in there."

He laughed, softly and close to her ear. "Some women enjoy having sex with other women."

"But do they not need a penis?"

More a chuckle than a laugh this time. She wasn't sure how much she liked his amusement at her lack of sexual knowledge.

"They find ways to compensate," he whispered against her neck. "You don't have lesbians on Acela?"

She shook her head. "We have nothing there. Careful genetic engineering is not conducive to . . . this."

A woman separated herself from the pile long enough to reach into a basket set nearby. She pulled out a tube and Ilyna leaned closer to the window, her curiosity peaked.

"I think you'll see one of those ways now," Bryan said. He was behind her, and his hands slid up over her thighs, the emerald satin bunching at her waist.

From the tube, the woman squeezed a glimmering gel into her fingertips. For a moment she rolled the lubricant on her fingertips, and then she grabbed the ankle of the woman nearest her.

She pulled the foot to spread the woman's legs, and then her hand disappeared between her thighs.

"Pity we don't have a better view," Bryan whispered.

Ilyna felt his hand sliding down her ass and relaxed her muscles, letting it slide between her legs.

She gasped when his finger slid into her. Clearly she was aroused, for her juices made no artificial gel lubrication necessary.

"They also use devices similar to yours," he was explaining, but she barely heard him. "Without the virtual reality."

Bryan's finger slid tortuously in and out of her and she couldn't stop the little whimper that escaped her lips.

He bit her earlobe and then slid another finger into her. "Would you like to try that?"

"I would miss your cock very much," she said, rocking her hips against his hands.

His fingers slid from her body, and she felt the head of his cock take their place. "You mean this, baby?"

She thrust back hard, impaling herself upon his erection. He groaned and tried to pull back, but she was already coming and she reached behind her to hold his hips against hers. When the tremors faded, Bryan pulled his still throbbing cock from her pussy and she sighed at the loss. The tip traced a moist trail around her clit, then it brushed delicately over her ass, pausing to rub not too insistently against the one place his body hadn't yet entered.

"Let's move to the next window," he whispered, and she smiled at the hoarseness in his voice. He was hanging on to his control by a thread, and she was going to make sure he lost it, no matter what tableau next greeted them.

BRYAN LED HER TO the next surveillance window, knowing this would be the last before his desire to come overcame his will-power. A threesome, he noted. Two males, one female. He wasn't so sure he wanted Ilyna carrying *ménage* images around in her over-active little imagination.

He realized the identity of the shorter blond man seconds before Ilyna did. He wasn't just blond. He was preternaturally pale—because his melanin was injected, not engineered, he re-called.

"Minister Jerrod," Ilyna whispered, her voice tight.

"I guess you're not the only Acelan with a secret," Bryan re-plied, trying to keep his tone light. He tried to nudge her toward the end of the hallway, but she wouldn't be moved. "Do you know the other man?"

"That is Cendrick, his aide. I don't recognize the woman, though."

"She works for Dane."

When Jerrod dropped to his knees in front of Cendrick, Ilyna

covered her mouth. For a moment Bryan thought she was crying, but when he leaned closer he realized she was trying not to
giggle. When the minister opened wide and accepted his aide's
entire cock deep into his throat, she lost the battle and laughed
out loud.

"He's pretty good at that," Bryan said. "He must practice . . . a
lot."

Cendrick moved his hips in a lazy rocking motion, sliding
his erection in and out of his boss's eager mouth. He looked almost bored, and Bryan was beginning to feel that way himself.
He stepped closer behind Ilyna and reached around to cover her
breasts with his hands. As he kneaded them, pausing occasionally
to tug at her nipples, Cendrick snapped his fingers at the woman
who'd up to that point only been watching.

Bryan felt Ilyna's breath quicken as Jerrod reclined on his back
on a low bench. He was afraid watching her minister engage in
sex would be too awkward for her, but her excitement hadn't
dimmed.

Cendrick poured oil into his hands, then made fists over Jerrod's erection, lubricating him until he glistened under the soft
lights. The woman straddled the minister, facing away, and Bryan's
own cock throbbed as Jerrod's slid into the woman's ass.

"Is he . . . oh my," Ilyna said, a ragged sigh escaping her. He
felt the tremble in her body, and he hooked one foot inside hers,
urging her legs farther apart. Bending his knees slightly, he rested
his length in the crack of her ass, letting her grow accustomed to
its feel.

"Do you want that, sweetheart?" he whispered into her hair.
"Do you want me to fuck your ass?"

She didn't answer, but she didn't pull away. Bryan looked back
at the window in time to see Cendrick step between the woman's

thighs. As the minster plunged his cock into the woman's ass, the aide pushed his own into her wet pussy. He imbedded himself to the hilt, then pulled back before plunging again, timing his thrusts with Jerrod's.

Ilyna's breath quickened, and Bryan pinched her nipple as punishment for being so excited by the sight of other men fucking. "Does that turn you on, Ilyna?"

"Oh, yes," she breathed. "Two cocks at once. It's . . . amazing."

Jealousy burned in his veins, and he reached into the pocket of his robe for the mini-bottle of lube. While he warmed it for a moment in one hand, he used his other to push gently on her shoulder blades while forcing her legs even farther apart. Then he pressed the head of his cock against her wet pussy and jammed it home. She gasped and had to grab on to the bar to keep from hitting the glass. He drove himself in to her right to his balls, hard, several times before pulling out of her entirely.

Then he poured the hot lube on his dick and touched the head against her virgin behind. If she wanted two cocks, he'd give her two cocks. But no other man was ever going to touch her again.

ILYNA STIFFENED WHEN BRYAN'S cock nudged at that tiny entrance, but she relaxed quickly. Bryan had given her nothing but pleasure and he wasn't going to change now. She watched the woman on the other side of the glass, could see her mouth forming words of encouragement, urging them on. The two cocks pounded into her and her breasts bounced and she appeared to be screaming with pleasure.

Taking a deep breath to relax herself, Ilyna pressed herself backward, meeting Bryan's careful thrust. There was an intense stretching sensation, a brief flash of pain, and then his cock was in her ass, gently fucking her. She whimpered and clutched the bar, letting this new sensation wash over her.

Bryan's breath was harsh and ragged, and she knew he was going to come soon. But he put his hands on her shoulders and pulled her upright against him. With his arm around her waist, he backed them up a pace or two.

"Put your feet up on the bar," he ordered, and with him supporting her weight she was able to rest her feet on the bar. The angle deepened the thrusts of his cock, and the pleasure bordering on pain almost drove her mad.

Then in the slight reflection of the glass, she saw what was in his left hand. She moaned, her body ready to come even before he held the vibrator up for her to see. "Suck on it, baby. Get it nice and wet because it's going in your pussy."

In the glass reflection, she made a big deal of running her tongue over the fake phallus and drawing it deep between her lips and Bryan's cock pulsed in her ass in response. On the other side of the mirror, the two Acelans had drawn away from the woman and now Ilyna watched as Cendrick bent over the bench and presented his own ass to Minister Jerrod, who proceeded to fuck his aide as if a man possessed by fury. She barely noticed when Bryan took the vibrator from her hand, but she noticed when it prodded the entrance to her pussy.

Her gaze returned to their own reflections and, positioned as she was, she could see Bryan fucking her ass even as he slid the warm metal into her. She was stretched and filled by the two cocks as they moved—sometimes in alternating strokes, sometimes in unison. Any thoughts of the trio in the private room fled and she could think of nothing but her own pleasure—her own image being fucked by two dicks.

Her muscles tensed and Bryan's hips quickened the pace while his hand slowed. When her orgasm came, she couldn't stop the scream, and as her body jerked against Bryan's she was aware of his own hard thrusts and guttural cry.

They landed in a panting, sweaty heap on the floor, and Ilyna made a promise to herself not to move anytime soon. She only sighed with contentment and wrapped her arms around his neck when Bryan finally lifted her into his arms and carried her back to their suite. He drew them a bath, and Ilyna was happy just to curl against his chest in the warm, sudsy water.

"Did I hurt you, honey?" he asked quietly, his cheek resting on the top of her head.

"No," she whispered. "It was a very pleasurable experience." She shrugged her shoulder. "But it didn't make me feel as . . . special as when we usually make love."

Bryan's arms squeezed her, and he pressed a kiss to her scalp. "You are special, Ilyna. You're very, very special to me."

She heard the sadness in his voice, but didn't quite understand where it was coming from. "Did I displease you tonight, Bryan? Because I enjoyed watching others having sex?"

"I'm not displeased. I'm worried that you'll want to stop watching and start joining in—that you'll get bored with me and want to enjoy new people or new experiences I can't give you. You have nothing to compare me to."

His heart was thumping rapidly under the flat of her hand, and Ilyna realized he was more than worried. Water churned and splashed as she turned to straddle him in the wide tub. She wanted to see his face.

"No, Bryan. I don't want anybody but you. Watching other people was fun, but you're the only one I want to make love with. I want to stay with you forever. We can leave here right now if it makes you worry."

He leaned closer until his forehead rested against hers. "We have to leave here soon, anyway. We've imposed on Dane long enough, and I have work commitments. I just . . . I just don't know where to go, sweetheart."

"It would be better for you without me, wouldn't it?"

He squeezed her again, this time so hard she almost couldn't breathe. "No. No matter what, it wouldn't be better for me without you."

He was lying, but he kissed her so tenderly she let it go . . . for now.

FOUR

THE TELEPHONE UNIT BEEPED discreetly, still set as it was on privacy mode. Bryan carried it as far from the bed as he could get so as not to wake Ilyna. "Hello?"

"They're coming for her," Dane said abruptly. "One of my bouncers—whose ass is fired, by the way—turned her in for the reward."

"But if we don't leave *Ris*-K—"

"According to the last interstellar treaty, an alien government can petition for the right to supersede our laws in a few extreme cases, one of which is the recovery of material possessions valued in excess of one hundred million Earth credits if the manufacturing of said possessions is unique or sensitive in nature."

"What does that have to do with us?"

"It's Ilyna, Bryan."

He glanced over at her, still curled in the center of the bed, fast asleep. There was no force on the planet—or off—that could make him give her up to the Acelan government. There had to be some kind of political asylum she could apply for.

"The Acelans made a case," Dane continued, "for her being a uniquely engineered material possession and our bastard president agreed. They can use force to get her back. You know I'd sacrifice all I've got for you and Ilyna, man, but I can't let my people get hurt."

"No, we're out of here. How long do I have?"

"Not long, but listen—"

"You've done all you can, Dane. I'll try to let you know somehow where we end up."

"You can't run, or you'll be running forever."

"I won't let them have her," Bryan hissed. "You don't know what they're going to do."

"I have a plan," Dane argued, but there was no way his big brother could get him out of this mess. Not without losing everything himself. "Trust me on this. Let her go with them for now and—"

"No!" Bryan interrupted, and Ilyna sat up on the bed, her eyes wide and frightened. "No way in hell. I'll be in touch."

"No, listen—"

Bryan disconnected the call and took a deep breath. He didn't want Ilyna to see his panic. Which was ridiculous as she was all too aware of the dangers she faced, but he still didn't want to add to her fear.

"We need to leave now, sweetheart."

He wouldn't have thought it possible for her eyes to open even wider, but they did, and then she was scrambling off the bed. "How long do we have?"

"I don't know, but not very long. We have to hurry." She was very still, and he wanted to stare at her forever, to memorize every inch of her.

She was so damn beautiful. Her regal bearing perfectly accented her body, which appeared to have been sculpted by a master. He may hate the sons of bitches, but he had to admit the Acelan scientists had done one hell of a job.

"Shouldn't we pack? Or . . . something?" she asked.

He walked to her, resting his hands on her bare shoulders. "There's no time. Put some clothes on, quickly, and let's go. We'll buy what we need later."

Still she didn't move. "Where will we go now?"

"I don't know, sweetheart. Someplace they won't think to look for us. It was obvious they would connect us to Dane, but I thought we'd be more secure here at Ris-K. Obviously I underestimated your government's desire to get you back."

He rested his forehead against hers, breathing deeply through his nose in effort to keep from plowing his fist into a wall. Why the hell would they invest so much in finding her just to make her a slave?

"Please get dressed, Ilyna," he whispered, unable to say everything he was feeling at the moment. "We need to go."

She slid a white sundress over her body, not even bothering with undergarments, and she was fishing for her second sandal when the door exploded into the room. Ilyna screamed and Bryan threw himself at her. She was scrambling toward him, sobbing, and he couldn't reach her.

Pain shot through his gut as a member of the Ambassador's Guard kicked him, and then two men grabbed his arms and pulled them behind his back. He tried to struggle, but they had the advantage. Another of the guards—all of them well armed, he noted—stepped to Ilyna and grabbed her arm.

"You will come with me now," he said in a flat voice.

She tried to touch Bryan's face as they went by, but her guard's grip on her elbow prevented even that small contact.

"I love you, Bryan, and it was worth the price."

The guard pulled her toward the door then, and Bryan renewed his struggle against the officers holding him.

"Don't hurt her, you bastards!" he shouted. "Don't you *fucking hurt her!*"

A fist hit him just above the nape of his neck and the blow drove him to his knees. The slight pinch of an injection, then the slamming of the door.

Ilyna.

With dark, blurry spots encroaching rapidly on his vision, Bryan reached for the phone.

IT TOOK MORE THAN a few favors called in on Dane's behalf to get them a five-minute audience with the Acelan minister. He was on his way back to his planet and didn't like being held up. Bryan didn't especially give a shit, and he wished desperately for a vidcam when Jerrod recognized him and his brother seconds after they entered the private room.

"Minister Jerrod, I've come for my wife."

"She is *not* your wife, Mr. Cameron. Ilyna is the Acelan ambassador to Earth. Your claim is ludicrous."

"Breed yourself another ambassador. Ilyna's staying with me."

Minister Jerrod stood, sweeping the creases from his robe with a practiced hand. "You are clearly delusional, and I am in a hurry. My security team is waiting to see you to your vehicle."

The minister started for the door, but Bryan reached out and grabbed his elbow. Jerrod flinched at the contact.

With his other hand, Bryan pulled his compact disc viewer from his pocket. "Is that any way to treat a fellow *Ris*-K aficionado?"

Bryan wouldn't have guessed the Acelan minister could get any paler, but he did. "I . . . you must have me confused with another, sir."

"Sure. What with all the short, albino-looking Acelans in the club, I guess it's possible."

Jerrod remained frozen for a moment, and then he jerked his arm. "I do not have time for games, Mr. Cameron. I must collect Ambassador Ilyna and return to Acela."

"You mean former ambassador, don't you?" Bryan stepped around to block the door.

Jerrod shook his head sadly. "Ilyna has disgraced herself and her people. She is . . . contaminated."

Blood rushed through Bryan's veins, throbbing in his ears like a cranked-up bass. He clenched and unclenched his fists, fighting the urge to put the Acelan ambassador through the wall.

"So you'll scar her," he said in a low, tense voice, "mutilate her and make her a slave."

"Our laws seem harsh to you, but we have to protect ourselves from the filth of your primitive society."

And the gloves were off. Bryan smiled and leaned back against the door. "How concerned were you about our primitive filth while you and your sidekick were fucking that blonde in *Ris*-K's VIP room?"

Dane snorted. "Forget fucking the blonde. It was the blow job that impressed me."

Jerrod's knees started to buckle, but the recovered himself quickly. "Get out."

Bryan hit Play and the room filled with the wet sounds of the Acelan minister sucking his aide's cock.

"How did you get this?" Jerrod cast an accusing glare at Dane. "You. The video feed is supposed to be secure and entirely confidential. There is legal precedent for not only a civil suit, but criminal action as well."

Dane shrugged. "So sue me. I'm sure you'll get off on the media

exposure. Bryan's my brother, asshole. Our blood may not be genetically homogenized for purity, but it matters."

The minister turned horrified eyes back to the screen, watching his own head bob up and down in full color, high resolution
glory.

"Your technique's a little boring, though. You may wanna try
some creativity next time. Some tongue action—"

Before Bryan could even react, Jerrod launched himself at
Dane, an eerie keening sound coming from the man's throat. The
alien minister never saw Dane's fist come up, but he sure as hell felt
it connect with his jaw.

He went down like a rock and Bryan rolled his eyes at his
brother. "I thought we were going to be civilized."

"Is he still breathing?"

"Yeah."

"Then I was civilized."

Bryan decided to shrug it off. Dane had a dark, empty place
inside him that was better left the hell alone.

Now they just needed the minister to regain consciousness so
they could resume their negotiations—so he could get his wife
back.

ILYNA SHIVERED ON THE floor of the holding cell, her head in
Myscha's lap as her friend stroked her head. The minister's first
petty act of retaliation had been the shearing of Ilyna's gorgeous
tresses, leaving a short mess of spiky blonde hair.

She didn't care, and the realization that, if he could see her,
Bryan wouldn't care either, had her sobbing even harder into her
friend's skirts. She had thought remembering Bryan would give
her strength, but it only intensified the horror of her loss.

"I'm sorry, Ambassador," Myscha whispered, and Ilyna felt a tear land on her temple.

"You must call me Ilyna now, and it's I who am sorry. He's going to find a way to make you pay for my transgressions as well, and it's not fair to you. You've always been loyal to me."

"And I always will be. Was it . . . was it wonderful?"

Ilyna sighed and rolled to her back, looking up at her friend. "It was more than wonderful, Myscha. *He* was more than wonderful. I don't know how our people have survived this long without feeling the things Bryan made me feel."

Myscha leaned her head down so Ilyna could hear her whisper, "If they leave us unwatched for even a moment, we should run."

The door opened in a sudden swish, and Ilyna jerked upright, certain that somehow they'd heard Myscha's words and had come to punish them. She nudged her former companion behind her, determined that nobody was going to hurt her friend, no matter what they did to her.

The bruised swelling on the minister's jaw stood out sharply against his white skin, and Ilyna wondered at its cause as she got to her feet, feeling Myscha do the same behind her. She lifted her chin, because they could strip her of her title, but they couldn't touch the person behind it.

A second later she realized the man behind him was Bryan and her stomach clenched in fear. What was he doing here? Did Jerrod plan to punish her by forcing her to watch her lover's torture? But Dane was behind them, and neither human looked overly anxious.

"I release you from your service to Acela," Minister Jerrod said formally, and she tried not to stare at the tic in his right eye. "You may never speak or act on behalf of the Acelan government in the future, nor return to Acela for the rest of your days. You are hereby banished forever."

Ilyna was speechless, her brain trying to keep up with the minister's words. Banished? He was letting her go? Why would he go to so much trouble retrieving her simply to release her again?

Bryan stepped around the minister and she collapsed into his open arms. "What's going on, Bryan?"

"After some rather sensitive negotiations, Minster Jerrod has agreed that you should be allowed to stay with your husband."

The bruise on Jerrod's jaw belied his words, but she didn't care. She squeezed Bryan until he pulled back to look at her. "I love your hair, sweetheart. It looks lighter and fun. You should dye it pink and tattoo my name across your ass."

"Leave now," Minister Jerrod hissed, stepping out of their path.

"What about her?" Dane jerked his head in Myscha's direction.

Jerrod's jaw tightened in a way that would have made Ilyna tremble if not for Bryan's closeness. "Myscha will be punished for failing at her assignment."

"Mutilation? Slavery?"

"Of course not. Myscha isn't contaminated. She was remiss in her duties, but she didn't betray her people."

Dane smiled, baring his teeth. "Try saying that with a mouth full of Cendrick's cum, Minister."

Jerrod's cheeks and neck reddened and Ilyna wanted to cheer as she realized the nature of their sensitive negotiations. "You, sir, are crude."

"And you, *sir*, are a hypocrite. Guess which I find more offensive."

"What will Myscha's punishment be?" Ilyna asked, stepping in before the two men came to blows.

Jerrod wouldn't look her in the eye. "She will spend some time in the kitchens, and henceforth be confined to Acela."

Ilyna's heart broke for her friend. "Myscha hasn't done any-thing wrong. Her job is . . . *was* to serve me."

Bryan slid his arm around her waist and pulled her close. "Let's leave this up to her. Myscha, do you want to return to Acela, or stay here with Ilyna?"

It wasn't Ilyna that Myscha's gaze went to as she considered, but Dane. Ilyna watched her watching the man and knew what her answer would be before she opened her mouth.

"I wish to stay with Ilyna," she said finally, looking down at her hands.

"Same terms," Minister Jerrod choked out, and then he swept from the room, his indignation lingering behind like a persistent bad odor.

The four of them were quiet for a moment, and then Myscha said quietly, "Are we really free?"

"Yes," Dane answered in a low voice. "The Acelans won't be interfering with either of you again."

"Where will I go?"

Ilyna turned to her friend, distressed by the plaintive note in her voice. Only minutes ago Myscha had been willing to run away with her. "Maybe you could stay at *Ris*-K for a while."

"That's not a good idea," Bryan said, obviously as aware of the sudden stiffness in his brother's shoulders as she was. "You were there with me, but I don't think the club's ready to have an unat-tached Acelan woman set loose in its midst. Dane's men would need riot gear. You can stay with us until you figure out what it is you want to do, Myscha."

"I have a place for her," Dane said, and Ilyna thought he looked surprised at having spoken. "A small, second-floor unit not far from Bryan's house. The woman who used to run *Ris*-K with me lives downstairs. She's quite advanced in age now, and you could look after each other. It's very secure, and it would help you and Ilyna put your old relationship behind you and grow as friends and equals."

Ilyna nearly cried at his kindness. "Oh, Myscha that's perfect!"

Bryan laughed and slugged his brother in the shoulder. "Very deep for a sex peddler."

Dane snorted. "And you sure get yourself in a shitload of trouble for an electrician."

"Can we go home now?" Ilyna asked, tucking her arm around Bryan's.

He nuzzled her hair, pressing a kiss to her scalp. "I can't wait to be back in my own house again—I mean, *our* own house."

"We can still visit *Ris*-K, though, right? Sometimes?"

His hand slid down to her ass, giving her a squeeze nobody else in the room could see. "On one condition—you marry me. I mean, the way we get married here on Earth."

"In Las Vegas?" Ilyna threw her arms around his neck and planted a kiss on his lips.

Bryan's fingers plunged into her hair as he deepened the kiss. Their breath mingled and his tongue danced lightly over hers. Only when Dane cleared his throat, did he pull away, and Ilyna was tempted to wrap her body around his, audience be damned.

"I don't care where we get married," Bryan whispered. "Las Vegas, Paris, the outer Milky Way, anywhere. When they took you from me . . . I love you, Ilyna."

"If I'm going to be an Earth wife, I need to start watching the cooking channel."

Bryan groaned and rubbed his stomach. "I'm going to need bigger pants."

FUTURELOVE

SUMMER DEVON

ONE

"COLLINS, YOU SMELL!" CHASE'S startled amusement woke Collins. He opened his eyes to find his fellow student leaning over his sleep mat. "I think you smell of sweat. Eh, what is with your face?" Chase lightly rubbed her thumb over the skin around his mouth. "There's hair on your chin! And cheek. Goes with all that head and brow hair you've grown lately. It's happening already. The *chlophim* has worn off."

Lying on his back, Collins suddenly became aware of Chase's fingers stroking his cheek. Another part of his body woke up and for the very first time in his life, Collins experienced an erection that did not go away after a few seconds. His lower belly tingled as strange longing whispered through him.

"Gah, you're right." He raised his head and looked down at his swelling penis with disgust. "I'm going into total wild state, no doubt."

"Good thing. Your assignment starts in less than two months. You'll need some practice for primitive removal . . . " Her voice petered out. "What is wrong with your penis?"

"Remember first-year training? Male symptom of wild state," he grunted.

"Oh." Chase's forehead furrowed. "That is amazing. It's so big." She reached down and touched him. "There's hair there too."

The brief stroke of her fingers made his cock jump. The tingling surged to a demanding thrum. Collins pushed her hand away and yanked his thin sleep cover over his torso. They all slept naked in the barracks, but for the first time in his life, Collins felt conscious of his nudity.

"Oops . . . sorry." Chase rose from her mat near his in the C-Unit training barracks. She trotted toward the waste disposal unit. "It's late. Instruction is about to start. Chin and Cane have already taken off."

His still erect organ throbbed almost painfully. He gingerly touched it the way Chase had. Good. An ache for more radiated from his loins.

Gah, he wouldn't join his fellow students with this object still offensively erect. They'd all been watching for his symptoms and would certainly have a lot to say about this one.

He brushed his fingers over it and experimented with a firmer touch. Unhampered by the suppression drugs, impatient nerve endings vibrated and demanded exploration. Even as his hand curled around the rigid member, he lay back on the mat and concentrated on recalling historical facts of his assignment's era. That might help distract him.

It didn't. Unfamiliar sensation coursed through him as his fingers slid over the large and suddenly alien part of his own body. Ah, forget distraction. It felt so very good to feed that hunger which still twisted through him, demanding satisfaction.

"Come on, get up," Chase shouted across the empty room. "You'll be late and you're the one who's traveling soonest. I know it's our favorite era, but which year are you heading for?"

"Two thousand . . . " Collins stopped talking when the fierce need in his crotch stole his breath. He could no more stop touching himself than he could fly. Unwilling to allow his physical self to take control, he struggled to speak. "Two thousand si-six."

Chase pulled the standard black agency uniform over her lean body and wandered over. She laughed. "Hoy, you still have that problem with your penis?"

"Argh," was all he could say. The memory of Chase's touch flooded him. His cock demanded it again. No, she wouldn't—couldn't—understand what she'd unleashed. He barely did. They'd learned about the wild state, but these sensations proved astoundingly powerful—far more distracting than he'd suspected from the dull explanations.

He rolled onto his side writhing with the strange wonderful tension but he froze as his newly rebellious body seized the last bit of control from his mind. Thick fluid pulsed from the blunt head of his penis. He stared at his hand and the odd mess in dismay. "Uck."

"Yeah." Chase wrinkled her nose. "I remember hearing about that in sexual sciences. I am not looking forward to going wild. Not a bit."

She turned and left the miserable, panting Collins to clean up.

He loved being a member of the elite time traveler division of the DHU but this had to be the worst side effect he'd ever experienced. Was he condemned to fight for control over his own body? He sighed and rolled onto his back. His heart still pounded behind his ribs, but the amazing fire had been extinguished, at least for the moment.

The disturbing yet undeniably pleasant vibrations abated. No wonder the men of ancient times had been slaves to their cocks. Did this sort of thing happen all day long? Collins threw on his clothes, determined to seek out a trainer in the history of sexual sciences as soon as he could.

He closed the manutabs on his uniform as he walked through the low-lit Spartan halls of the agency complex. Yes, the peculiar episode was disquieting but he reminded himself he still had time to learn to deal with this nuisance. And his assignment would last only two days. Even though he'd be in a small city he wouldn't have to encounter any people. Good thing—he recalled from his first year of time travel agency training that females could pose a problem to a wild-state male.

Females. The word seemed to chime through him.

No. That soft thrum through his body was the implanted internal alarm that told him he was late for his first session.

Bah, his captain would give him trouble again—

A thudding explosion ripped the air. Collins threw out a hand for balance as the floor shook. His annoyance vanished, replaced by startled dread.

Years of training kicked in. His hand went to his side, groping for a weapon. Not there. Gah, he'd left it behind in his hurry. The blasted erection episode had weakened his thinking.

He waited, confused thoughts swirling through him. Who would want to attack the DHU? The anti-timeys were a joke, weren't they? No one could seriously doubt the importance of the agency's travelers. The marks of their journeys back in history were written all over the past. They were necessary to keep mankind alive through the darkest ages.

The beat of running footsteps grew near. He crouched, ready for hand-to-hand combat. One of his training agents came careening around the corner. Ash smudged her cheek and blood showed through tears in her uniform. "Collins. Good!" Mostan panted, her panicked eyes wide. "Come on."

She clutched his arm and yanked him through the nearest doorway. The travel chamber.

Mostan breathed so hard he had trouble understanding her. "Your assignment. They're going to try to stop you. They'll kill you. Go now."

He tried to shake her off. "But I'm not a full agent. My training isn't—"

"Who are they? Who's attacking us?"

"Go." She shoved him toward the silver disk of the travel platform. She was pushing him back into the past.

The unfamiliar spinning already seized him. "My return," he shouted. "No one has—"

A fog of energy rolled across the platform, covering his eyes. In the unlocked doorway, a misty group of figures appeared. They appeared to be grappling with the trainer and pushing her aside. The swirling power field built quickly and dragged at him.

He recognized an attacker—his unit-mate Chin. She screamed at Collins but he couldn't make out her words over the roar of the force now ripping into the chamber.

A fist bashed into Collins's face. *Chin's?* Stunned by the blow and blinded by the increasing field, Collins pulled himself all the way onto the platform and pressed the release. The spinning and pain seized him and battered him through time. No travelers' aid tablet eased his passage. He clutched his pounding head and mercifully passed out.

2006

CANDY LISTENED AS HER mother's voice echoed from the answering machine in the kitchen.

"Are you screening your calls again, Candy? Candy!"

Damn, she hated her own name. She and her sister Cookie agreed that if they ever managed to leave Springfield, they'd take on sophisticated names like Gabrielle and Gwen.

No names that ended with "y." No names of food or drink or flowers.

"Candy? You promised everyone at the reunion that you'd think about moving back if you didn't get a better job. Well? Sam has been very patient and we think that—"

She gave in and picked up the phone. The answering machine beeped off. "Mom, I know. I've got a couple of interviews and—"

"But what about Sam?"

"That's between Sam and me."

"Sam and I," her mother corrected, incorrectly.

"Right, Mom. Between us."

"But I swear he's pining for you, hon. And he's a good man—you could do a lot worse."

Candy shouldn't have bothered to pick up the call.

She managed to get her mother off the phone before she lost her temper but not before she developed the need for a very stiff drink.

She grabbed her denim jacket to head out of the apartment for the bar two blocks away. After work the sidewalks were empty except for the occasional baby stroller-and-mom combination or homeless people. No Prince Charming strolled beneath the shade of the raggedy elms, darn it all.

Not that she required much in a guy. Sam made her laugh and his kisses . . . well, they were competent but her mind tended to wander during them. He wasn't head over heels about her either but being head over heels wasn't a priority for him, he'd explained.

They'd been good friends so long—even Sam had begun to think they'd get married someday.

The warm evening soothed her and she decided that rather than get drunk, she'd go for a walk. She could practice being a contented spinster by sitting on a bench in the park and—she checked herself—no, not feeding ducks. A contented spinster reading the sign about not encouraging wildlife by feeding them.

The trouble was if she wanted to remain single she'd have to work at it. Maybe make her mother lose confidence in her. What if someone at home caught her with a man—someone who wasn't Sammy. One night as they split a bottle of wine, she and Sam had made a halfhearted not-entirely-serious pact to marry if they hadn't found anyone else in a couple of years. When Candy had mentioned it to her mother, Mom had decided it was a real engagement.

If she could show up at her mother's house with a man in tow, Mom might give up her Sam plan.

She tucked her feet up on the bench and morosely contemplated a flock of pigeons. Something thudded down next to her.

Jamming herself against the arm of the bench, she stared. A man. A large disheveled man in a strange black getup.

She jumped to her feet. For a wild moment she wondered if she'd managed to summon him with her thoughts. But then her instincts kicked in. She suddenly grew aware that a big male stranger had landed way too close.

"What the heck are you doing?" She backed farther away. "There are seventy benches in this damn park and . . . oh . . ."

He pressed his palm against his forehead and closed his eyes. A dark smear of blood marred his cheek.

She gasped and covered her mouth with her hand. "Are you all right?"

He gazed at her. She met perfect hazel eyes in a perfect

face. Too perfect. He gave a slow nod. "I think I've been what is called . . . er . . . mugged."

He gave a soft groan and more blood trickled down the side of his face.

"Damn," she yelped. "Hold on. We gotta call the police."

She opened her woven bag, scrabbled through it looking for her cell phone.

"No." A very large, very strong hand grabbed hers. "No, give me a moment. I shall recover and be on my way."

He had the oddest flat accent. Scandinavian perhaps. The faint color drained from his face and he looked pale—bordering on grey.

"Hey, are you about to faint? Should I call an ambulance?"

He waved a hand at her. "No, please do go about your business, madam. I promise I shall return to normal soon."

If he ever had been normal . . . Her rude thought shamed her. Jeez, poor guy, visiting from another country and getting mugged? "At least let me help walk you to the hospital or something. It's only a few blocks from here."

Collins had the worst headache he'd ever experienced and the indigenous female would not go away. If he could walk to this hospital, perhaps she would leave him. He could get on with his task. A relatively easy one. He hadn't traveled in the routine manner but he had the training to carry out his duty.

His job of thwarting a near-murder didn't involve much interaction—new agents only got simpler assignments. He gave a furtive glance at the female next to him. Too bad the agency hadn't done enough research. This assignment apparently took place in a small city in which natives seemed to notice one another. Not like everyone's favorite easy location of this era, New York. The worst agent wouldn't be detected there.

He tottered to his feet and suppressed a groan. If only he could use a quick response tab for traveling, but he didn't have one. Travel accounted for only part of the nausea hitting him. Mostan had pushed him into this assignment early. Was she all right? The agency . . .

He had to quash unfamiliar emotion. Panic would not help. He must concentrate on his task and then try to figure out what had happened back at the DHU. Was there an agency to pull him back to his time? No. He would wait until he was alone to focus on such disturbing thoughts. First he needed to find out if he could fulfill his assignment.

The woman stood too. She was tall for her time but short for his. For a moment he allowed himself to be distracted by his first encounter with a genuine native.

Her loose brown hair flowed around the edges of her face and fell across her shoulders. DHU agents who had hair wore it in a universal cropped style. Her small waist, rounded hips—all evidence of natural unsuppressed development and beautiful in an uncivilized sort of way. Odd, he wouldn't have thought he'd find such untamed disarray so . . . intriguing.

Strange sensations assaulted him as he noticed her body. She had the exaggerated mammary glands of her time as well. But for some reason he did not find this natural appearance ludicrous or unattractive. Instead, he wondered what they might feel like in his hands. His curiosity sharpened. The hunger awoke and so did his penis.

"Quit staring at my boobs," she said breathlessly.

He quickly looked down and concentrated on staring at the grey surface of the walking path. He hadn't had enough training for this. He had to get away from her. "I beg your pardon. I do not wish to be rude."

"Yeah, right. Listen. You're too beat to walk that far. I forgot my cell phone but I live right over there, a ten-minute walk. Less. Wait here and I'll call for help."

"You are very kind." What was the expression they used here? *Not a chance in hell.* "I'm slightly confused. Would you tell me the date?"

She hesitated. "May fifth."

"Ah." His assignment fell on May sixth—but he didn't want to ask the year.

Her brow furrowed. "You're confused? That's a sign of concussion."

"I do not have a concussion."

She put her hand on his shoulder and he caught her scent. DHU agents complained about the harsh smells of the past but her fragrance was actually pleasant. A light flowery perfume, perhaps? To cover the wild-state musk? Unsuccessful. It didn't hide a tantalizing scent. He drew in a deep breath to savor the underlying fragrance. He could almost taste her and—

"Hey, you're still bleeding. I can't leave you here. Can you walk a couple of blocks? Maybe I should look for a cab."

"I'll walk." While they walked, he might figure out some way to disengage her attention. A chance to practice ignoring this peculiar attraction as well.

He silently followed her along a path to a tall building. She reached for the double glass doors.

Attempting a smile, he ignored the dizziness. "I feel much better and I would prefer not to go to a doctor."

"Okay, but let me at least get you an Advil or something. I can tell you're in pain."

She pulled open the doors and at the back of the big entrance hall, she started up some concrete stairs. He followed her up the stairs, trying not to watch her rear end. "Ought you allow a stranger in?"

She twisted around and scowled down at him. "Damn, I didn't know you were there. Listen, don't get any ideas. I have a big old dose of pepper spray in my bag and—oh!"

Her hands flailed the air. Her feet flew up. She tipped backward, and thumped down. Right into his arms.

He caught her easily and continued up the stairs, clutching her to his chest. A delicious warm weight. *Put her down*, he commanded himself.

Not yet. She might fall again.

The feel of her in his arms disconcerted him. His right hand cradled her warm, bare thighs where her skirt had hiked up, and his left hand . . . If he stretched those fingers perhaps he might stroke the outer curve of her breast. He'd never been this close to another human except during sleep or training and that grappling on the matted floors had no effect on him. Oh this most certainly did.

And what about the implications of saving a woman who might have been slated to fall? Convoluted thought and sensation whirled through him—this wild state seemed to have scrambled his brain permanently.

She began to yelp indignantly. "Omigod. It's fake. You're not really hurt. You couldn't have caught me without doing yourself in."

He'd reached the top of the stairs. The wooziness threatened to overwhelm him.

The woman's tone switched from indignant to concerned again. It seemed to be a habit with her. "Hey. What's wrong? You're turning white."

He put her down and sank onto the top step hoping he wouldn't pass out.

No fraternizing. Only terrible agents committed heinous

crimes such as making too much contact with indigenous folk un-related to the assignment.

The very worst time travel agent in fifty years of agency history. He covered his face with his hands.

"Did you say something?" The woman hovered over him.

"No. Nothing." Gah, had he spoken some of his thoughts out loud? Thank goodness she hadn't understood. With some relief, he recalled that speaking one's thoughts was a temporary travel symptom. Temporary. Maybe the hunger to draw near to this woman was another symptom.

Her white and pink footwear—running shoes, were they called?—filled his vision. "Listen, I'm sorry I yelled. You startled me because you're so quiet. I think . . . You might have saved my life."

She let out a whoosh of air. "Wow. I need to sit down too." She gawked down the stairs and then dropped next to him on the top step. "You know what? That was amazing. I really would have taken a tumble if you hadn't been behind me. Maybe both of us could have done a Jack and Jill act. Of course maybe I wouldn't have fallen if I hadn't tried to act tough."

He straightened and looked at her. Large dark brown eyes caught and held his gaze. She smiled. The luminous eyes caused internal commotion.

He could feel his penis respond. It pressed against the cloth of his uniform. Emotion no longer centered in his brain. His whole body tingled. He longed to touch her. Other strange acts he vaguely recalled mentioned in his studies crowded his mind. His weird instincts focused upon this female.

Oh please no.

She still wore a crooked, uncertain smile as she turned and leaned close to him. Her sweet breath touched his cheek.

This was entirely wrong, yet intriguing to be so very near a native of this era. Her face almost brushed his as her eyes closed and her lips parted. He moved away. Without thinking, he reached out and gently stroked her mouth with his forefinger. Warm and so very soft. Now her gentle exhalation brushed his hand. His mouth went dry.

She pulled back and his fingers missed touching her plump mouth.

The woman shook her head and her golden skin flushed red. "You're a nice guy. That's a lovely way to tell me to stop."

"Stop what?" He wondered at his own breathlessness. Certainly carrying her weight up the stairs would not cause respiratory distress.

"Stop me from kissing you." She smiled briefly then grew serious again. "I swear I'm not usually such a-a hussy. I've never had the urge to kiss a total stranger. Before, I mean."

"Ah." He knew about kisses—mouths mimicking nursing babies and a gesture of affection. A repulsive germ-spreading habit. There were practitioners of course, though not among the elite agency trainees or other military personnel.

But he was in wild state and the woman's full lips glistened. The idea of touching his lips to hers made his heart beat faster and caused another surge of . . . lust. He remembered the proper name of the primitive emotion at last.

Oh no. Never. Not an indigenous. Trouble . . .

His implanted internal reminder did not work in this era or it would have been screaming, shaking him to pieces.

He stood. "I am better. No need to go to the medical facility."

On top of the blasted lust he still had other problems. He forced himself to keep his eyes open. Without the right medication, the post-travel symptoms would last for another few hours.

The need for sleep draped like a heavy blanket over him and he wondered if he swayed.

The female climbed to her feet. She watched him as if he was fascinating. Had anyone ever observed him like this? Not even the medicos during exams. Mingling with the panic was the reckless desire he had never experienced. Meeting her gaze only increased his powerful and confusing wild-state sensation. He could not allow them to overwhelm his mind.

She spoke and even the strange singing cadence of her words seemed to wrap him in the peculiar hunger to touch her. "You look kind of beat. Come on in and rest at least."

"No." He shook his head and smiled in what he hoped was an apologetic manner. He had to escape this woman and her effect on him.

"Come in or I'll call 911. I'm worried about you."

Nine-one-one. It did not sound good. He could manage to enter her home if it would keep her from raising any kind of alarm. For a short time, he reminded himself. He had to face the wild state and this woman—but only for the shortest possible time.

TWO

OLLINS FOLLOWED THE NATIVE through the door. She had a quaint dwelling and he recognized the style his history trainer called Student Eclectic.

"Cindyblock." He pointed at the bookshelf. On the shelf sat a small calendar. His heart soared.

The date was right.

Despite the strange incident at the DHU and the peculiar hurry, he'd been shoved back to the correct year.

"Oh yeah." She wrinkled her nose. "Cinder blocks and boards. Not exactly elegant. Well, I didn't know how long I'd be here. Come on and sit down on the couch. Let me get you a towel and some water or something."

Fascinated, he watched as she carelessly poured a big glass of pure water.

"Thank you," he said reverently. "Oh, it looks delicious."

"Just water." She laughed and he knew he'd shown ignorance again.

He took the bumpy bit of cloth she called a towel and pressed it to his head. When she handed him the glass, he couldn't help gulping it down and marveling at the cool slide of water down his throat. As much pure water as he wanted. This strange era seemed full of spectacular sensations—taste, touch, smell, things his physical being longed to explore. He would not give in, though these new urges intrigued him.

He smiled at her. "Thank you. Where I come from there is little plain water for drinking. It must be used for other purposes." Now why did he say that? He'd at least stopped himself from adding only the very rich can afford flavorless unadulterated fluids.

Her lush mouth tightened as she directed another furrowed, curious glance at him. "You seem better but that's got to hurt. I'll get you some ice."

"No need. I will rest for a few minutes and be on my way."

He'd landed in the right year. All other concerns could wait hours. Relief flooded him even as his eyes closed without his permission and he fell sideways as if a terrific force pulled him over.

Trainers underplayed the description of travel's effects or maybe they hadn't experienced it without taking aids. The indigenous female might well have saved him. If he'd passed out like this in a public area what could have hap—

The world went black.

CANDY PEEKED UNDER THE ratty towel. The man's bleeding had stopped and color touched his cheeks and mouth. Candy had contemplated calling for help but decided he was only asleep and he'd be okay. Way better than okay in fact. She inspected the most gorgeous male she'd ever seen and entertained herself by making wild guesses about him. Maybe he was some kind of cover model or something. Despite the fact that she was unimpressed by men who made their living by showing off their good looks, she couldn't help being impressed by his appearance.. She searched for signs of plastic surgery. No, that straight nose and chiseled perfect mouth probably just grew there. Wow. Talk about luck of the draw.

The lines of his broad shoulders and flat belly had to be the result of strenuous workouts.

What strange black trousers and shirt he wore. Absolutely plain, tight as a T-shirt, but some kind of shining almost glittering thin fabric. Eww, maybe he was Eurotrash.

Even his short pale hair glowed—a combination of wheat and gold. No doubt he kept it moussed.

She leaned closer and discovered the hair was matted with blood but not stiff with hair products. The short strands slipped through her fingers, soft and smooth. He slept, even as she touched his hair, face and silken clothing. What if he did have some sort of concussion? Weren't you supposed to wake people up when they'd gotten bashed on the head?

She knelt by him and brushed his shoulder. He didn't flinch. No, she wouldn't shake him. That would probably be bad for someone who'd thwacked his head.

"Hey, mister," she shouted into his ear.

His eyes opened at once. He folded upright, his magnificent abs flexing visibly beneath the thin fabric. He winced.

"I want to make sure you aren't concussed," she explained.

Something like fear came and went in the hazel eyes. "No," he whispered. "No. I'm not. I assure you."

She rose to her feet. Wow, he was tall. Even seated on the low couch his head was level with her breasts.

"Look, maybe you should go to the hospital."

"No, I assure you that I am not badly hurt. It would be a waste of time."

He had a point about time. A month ago her friend Kathy had gotten the flu and they had spent more than four hours in the emergency room on a slow night. She had no urge to repeat that kind of wait and she wouldn't dump him on his own.

"Can I give you a lift to your hotel?"

He shook his head then grimaced. "Much of my trouble is that I am tired. I have recently . . . traveled a great distance. If you would not mind, might I just rest for a short while?"

She rubbed her eyes. "Okay then sleep again. I'll just wake you up every now and then to make sure you don't have a concussion. That a deal?"

"You do not need to trouble yourself." He smiled. Had he done that before? The smile was so beautiful—a flash of perfect white in his perfect tanned face—she felt resentment. How dare anyone be that appealing? She waved a hand at the couch. "Sleep."

He nodded then winced again. Even furrowed those perfect brows looked attractive. "Thank you. I am most grateful."

He sank sideways and fell asleep at once. She fidgeted, unwilling to move away from him. If the stranger caused this much fuss inside her while he slept, wow—imagine him awake and healthy.

Holy shit, she was alone with a peculiar stranger in weirdo clothes. Did his straight-backed posture say anything about him? Military? Dancer? Or just the kind of guy who examined himself in the mirror for hours until he got the right poses for his superb body?

The stresses of the day finally hit her and she yawned. Hmmm. Her couch, really a daybed, was exceptionally large. Plenty of room for two people lying on their sides. And she'd be prudent to keep an eye on the man in case he went into convulsions or something. She might as well be comfortable.

She rested her butt on the edge of the couch and gingerly stretched out so that she lay next to him. Though their bodies did not touch, his heat reached her breasts, belly and her thighs.

There.

Okay, but not too comfortable—for one thing, she was balanced on the edge of the sofa. For another, she lay within a hairsbreadth of the most attractive man she'd ever seen—a man so strong he'd carried her up the stairs as if she weighed no more than a bag of groceries. And she'd attempted to kiss this guy. What had she been thinking?

Not thinking. Feeling. Her skin prickled, impatient to have the stranger's strong hands move over it. Her nipples had tightened to aching beads when he'd carried her. He'd been so close to touching her breast she'd almost twisted in his arms for the feel of his fingers there. She sensed he'd wanted to, yet held himself back. Better than she had with her clumsy attempt at kissing.

No, wait—with those looks and that body. She wondered if he was gay.

She sat up for another long, leisurely examination of the injured stranger. His mouth parted slightly and she heard deep, even breathing. He had a sexy mouth, the lower lip a little fuller than the top. Wide and mobile. And kissable. Two hours and she'd wake him. Maybe look into those pale hazel eyes—strictly to see if the pupils reacted normally, of course. She settled next to him, determined to remain awake.

COLLINS WOKE AT ONCE from the deepest sleep he'd had in years. He froze. Deep cushions, not his mat, cradled his weight. The room was nearly black and they did not have total darkness in the C quarters. He was used to waking with a body sleeping next to him but though he could not see this person, he knew she was not Chase. A foreign exotic scent invaded his senses. Too earthy and . . . heady.

Vibrations seemed to radiate from her. From him too. Even in his sleep he'd matched his breath to the person—the very, very female being—lying next to him.

His body responded with full wild-state arousal. Blood surged to his stiffening cock, to his fingertips—his body vibrated with need.

The vibrations coursed through him. *Touch her. Taste her. This is what you need. This. Right here. Reach for her.*

He pushed against the cushions behind him and tried to sit up without disturbing her. Surely her quarters had other rooms. Maybe he needed to empty his bladder? Perhaps that accounted for the rigid state of his penis?

No such luck. All of the extreme response centered on the woman. He squeezed his hands shut to block the tingling. *Stroke her skin. Warm. Soft.*

She wiggled closer and he breathed in her scent. So primitive and unlike the grassy chemical scent he knew from his own time. He lay back down. As he inhaled deeply, he hoped the dizziness he felt lingered from the travel.

"Mmm," the sleeping female murmured and wrapped her arm around his torso.

She shifted closer. He stopped breathing. Her yielding body's heat touched him. Her hand rested on his back and her breasts pressed against his chest. Firm nipples nudged him through the thin fabric of his uniform. So much contact all at once. The wicked unfamiliar hunger attacked him, hitting hard.

No, no, no, no, no.

He must have groaned aloud. She shook her head so that strands of her hair brushed his face.

"Hey," she said as she yawned. "I fell asleep. Sorry. You okay?"

He'd expected her to move, back away angrily, perhaps accuse him of lascivious thoughts. Fairly obvious with that troublesome organ right on the front of his body advertising his attraction. Her warm thighs pressed against his erection and he held back a groan of pleasure at the contact.

Instead of protesting or moving away from his aroused body, she reached up and brushed his forehead with her fingertips. Gah, who knew the contact of skin against skin could cause the hunger to grow. Lust urged him to discover her texture and shape. He clenched his fists until his nails bit his palms. Maybe pain would keep from responding to her gentle, exploring touch.

"What's your name?" she whispered.

"Collins."

He could sense her smile in the darkness. See it actually for his eyes had adjusted to the light coming through the chinks in the curtains.

"That's an English name," she said and her hand continued to stroke his skin, his hair. "I thought you were from somewhere like Denmark or something."

He didn't answer. His whole being concentrated on the tingle of her touch on his forehead and his cheek. Warmth shimmied through him.

"I'm Candy." She gave a quiet laugh. She did seem amused by the world. Was that typical of the indigenous here? "I forgot I want to inform the world that my name is Gabrielle. Oh well, born a Candy, die a Candy."

"Do you often change your names?" he asked, glad for a distraction. "I mean people like you?"

She snorted—a sound of derision no doubt. "If you had the name Candy you'd change it."

"Candy." It rolled over his tongue as delicious as sugar and other illegal delights. Mouthwatering forbidden treats. "I like this name," he said and wondered why he volunteered the fact.

"Oh. Well." Her laughter this time sounded nervous. "Thanks."

She shifted her hips and renewed awareness of the contact of their bodies charged through him, particularly at his aching groin.

"Oh." The sound escaped him without his permission.

Could he sneak off and get rid of the distracting sensation? From his recollection of that first episode, all he had to do was rub himself and eventually it diminished. Not before making a bit of a mess. Evacuation. That was the name of it—no, not quite—but close. Gah, he wished he'd paid better attention to his sexual science trainers.

Her hand tentatively caressed his neck now and he closed his eyes to try to escape the arousal she caused. He'd allowed himself enough time with this female. Certainly he'd nearly recovered from the travel and could make his way to the assignment location.

He'd concentrate on the mission. That would help him pull away from her. He'd done years of training for the brief moment. *Don't blow it. Do the mission.*

After he finished his assigment . . . at least he knew his return coordinates and he'd just wait for that, too.

Her hand slid to his shoulder and proved too distracting. The stir caused by her warm hand rubbing his aware flesh disturbed and intrigued him. Surely she was some sort of expert at these sexual sciences. Her gentle touch on him at once soothed and jangled every nerve in his body. He tried not to think of how he yearned to have her rub his painfully erect cock in that manner. Every inch of him wanted her touch.

She shifted and another softer warmth brushed his cheek—her breath and then her lips. His eyes snapped open.

She smiled but then raised her eyebrows in an odd grimace.

"You're gawking at me like I just drove a knife between your ribs. I—I just went with the moment."

"But," he said hoarsely. "No. Ah."

He thought he saw her eyes roll. "I know, I know. It was a stupid impulse—I don't usually do that kind of thing. Sorry. You don't have to look as if I'd violated you or anything. It was just a quick kiss."

"A kiss?" He'd thought they only occurred mouth to mouth.

"Yup. Nothing scary."

That's what you think. Oh gah, perhaps he'd spoken his thought aloud again. He had to escape, avoid any contact at least until he was back to full functioning.

The couch creaked as she pushed herself up on an elbow. "You're scared of kisses?"

Her scent reached him—the musk of pure Candy beneath the scent of flowers. Nothing in his world had ever caused his mouth to water before but now he raged with hunger.

"No, of course I'm not."

Those dark eyes made an unnerving scrutiny. "Yes, you are. You're scared of kisses." She bit her lower lip and in a quiet voice asked, "Are you gay? Or in a committed relationship?"

"No to both of your questions." Why did he answer? He must leave before he made an even more stupid mistake. "But I'd best get going now."

"Oh. Okay." She rolled—and promptly fell off the couch and landed with a thud on the ground.

"Are you hurt?" He leaned over to look at her.

She laughed. "Nah, not even my pride."

She climbed to her feet and held out a hand. He frowned at it. "I'm helping you up. Nothing sinister," she said, a trace of impatience in her low voice.

His chilled fingers enveloped her warm hand as he quickly slid from the couch and stood.

Oh, the newly sensitized skin of his hand tingled with the need to explore the fascinating warmth of her. He could not let go or he might give in to the urge to touch her round, sweet feminine face. The shocking presence of another human. So close.

"You feel it too," she whispered, sounding as stunned as he felt. "I-I don't remember ever being so immediately attracted to someone." She squeezed his hand and gave a quick grin, a gleam of white in the dark. "But I bet you get that sort of come-on line all the time."

He shook his head.

His body urged him on again. *A kiss. Experience it. You can't call yourself an expert on an era when kisses were important unless you know what it means to kiss.* He knew justification when he heard it, even when his own body and brain coerced him.

Fine, just a kiss, he thought to shut up the stupid urges. Only one, before he'd get home and put himself on the blessed *clophim* suppressant.

Gah, yes—the moment he got back, he'd gulp down a double dosage. No way he could control this . . . attraction. *Then why try? Why not indulge for another minute?*

He inched closer, still holding her hand.

No one would ever know. He found himself croaking the words, "Just one kiss. Before I go."

Candy pulled her hand from his so she could cup his face. Inwardly she groaned. Why couldn't she just leave the man alone? He'd made it clear that, despite his arousal, he didn't want this. But she almost had to touch him, kiss him. God, it would be something to remember as an old lady sitting on a park bench watching ducks. The day she kissed the most good-looking man on the planet.

She'd once read the line "throbbing tension between them" and had scoffed at the phrase, but something throbbed between them—and not just between her legs.

Even in the dark room she could make out that mouth. Chiseled, warm and wonderful. He seemed to be waiting for her to move to him. She angled her head and grazed his lips once, twice, with her own. Before she could really settle in, he spoke.

"Oh." His deep voice was husky. "That is nice."

His startled pleasure, the way he'd not opened his mouth—and she suddenly understood.

The man had never kissed anyone.

How could that be?

She held back her surprise though, figuring any male would be insulted if she expressed amazement.

"Yes," she whispered. "Hold on to your horses, there's more."

"But—" he murmured before she licked her lips and brought her mouth onto his again.

Tentative at first, sweet, delicious. Sensations rather than words rolled through her as their uncertain contact strengthened. She flicked the tip of her tongue over his full lips and his mouth opened. A small whimper rose from her throat and met his answering groan. She wrapped her arms around his surprisingly wide and hard torso.

Good, his tongue hesitantly brushed hers. She sucked his lip lightly. A moment later he imitated her. Good gravy, she grew heady with the realization that she played teacher to the best-looking man on the planet.

He twisted and seemed almost to try to escape, but she lightly tipped her pelvis against him, seeking out that incredible huge stone-hard ridge of his cock. Wow, through the thin cloth she felt his heat and the very shape of him. He wore nothing else. His arms went around her and his lips met hers again.

His mouth broke away at last and he leaned his head back, panting. Aha, nice throat. She nibbled kisses onto his superb neck. So maybe he used moisturizer or something to have skin that soft. She wasn't in the mood to criticize the man just now.

"Just the kiss." He might have been begging. His fingers pressed on either side of her spine. Despite his tone, he pulled her closer. "Just one."

She didn't protest but knew one kiss would not be enough.

She flicked her tongue over his throat and pressed her mouth to his pulse.

Shy Candy, her friends called her. Not anymore. No sirree, not when she had a prize like this. For a moment she almost laughed. Turnabout, she decided. She knew how it felt to be considered a piece of meat. Plenty of times in the past men had hungrily stared at her breasts or legs.

She didn't want to hurt him. Heck, she just wanted to see as much of the astounding man that she could. Exchange a few more kisses, maybe?

Bull.

She wanted more of him. Her breasts, her pussy—even her toes—ached with astounding desire. She wanted this man more than she'd longed for anything in her life. The need to run her hands over his smooth skin was so strong it almost frightened her. She imagined him pumping hard and deep inside her and both of them out of control.

Yes, a nice fantasy, but she would settle for kisses.

So many reasons to let go and wave good-bye. Sex with a stranger? Really, really bad idea—even for this new desperate and starving Candy. And if she could get past that . . . problem . . . she had no condoms and she could pretty much guarantee this guy didn't either.

She stroked his hair. He turned his head and pressed his mouth to the palm of her hand. A small mew of pleasure rose from her throat at the stir of his breath.

Okay, she offered up her conscience a compromise and a sacrifice. She'd give up coffee and chocolate for a chance at seeing him without clothes. Heck, she'd move back home even, if he'd let her touch his skin.

Her conscience responded. *When did you become such a brainless tramp? Who is this man?*

She wished her conscience would shut the hell up.

Her mouth found his again, and at once they launched into lush, urgent kisses. He learned fast. No hint of awkwardness or hesitation as his tongue and lips explored her mouth and at last his hands began to move over her back and bottom.

Oh, yeah. She rubbed herself against him. Now was not the time to worry. Regrets came after, not before. And dammit, she needed something to regret for those long days as a spinster.

She let go of him for a moment to reach over and turn on the dimmer on the lamp by the couch. Just a low glow so she could see him.

"Wow," she whispered.

He stood in the middle of the floor, watching her, his arms folded over his chest. The thin clothes didn't do much to hide his erection, though he did not seem to notice. His face looked stern, but she didn't miss the parted mouth and the way his chest rose and fell rapidly.

"Just stay a few minutes, before you go?" She abandoned all pride and grabbed at his hand.

"A few." He gently pulled his hand from hers and traced the line of her mouth. His grim expression relaxed. "I think there is a saying? In for a pence?"

She nodded. "In for a penny in for a pound."

"Hmmm, that must be it. But I shan't go all the way to the pound, do you see?" He cleared his throat, but still his voice came low, ragged, "A kiss. More kisses. For your mouth is so very delicious. It is worth the trouble."

"No trouble," she assured him.

"I shall leave and you will not see me again."

"Yeah, I got that idea." She scrubbed her hand over her mouth as if trying to drive out the desire. At least he was honest.

She framed his face with her hands and pulled him down to taste his mouth. Clean and luscious . . . the banked-back urgency of the kiss grew with the stroke of tongues. As his solid body pressed against her, her mind did indeed wander, but not to her to-do list. Her mind wandered straight to new and erotic territories that involved this man naked, on top of her, between her legs. Yum.

Candy pulled away, gasping, and edged back to the couch, her hand clutching his thick wrist. She patted the seat next to her. He frowned and didn't move.

"We can just talk," she said, faltering.

The frown turned into a gorgeous incandescent smile. "Now that would be even worse," he muttered.

"What? You a murderer or something?" She laughed. Then again, someone had attacked this guy in the park. Maybe it had been a brawl and he wasn't a passive victim.

"No, I haven't hurt anyone." He sank down next to her so gracefully, she wondered if perhaps he was a dancer. A Chippendale—or more likely ballet dancer, since he had so easily caught her as she'd fallen on the steps. Or a really slick hired killer? Man, she watched too much television. She didn't think she needed to be worried about the guy who'd saved her from a bad tumble. But still she pondered aloud, "Should I be afraid of you?"

He shook his head. "No, not at all."

"So why not talk?"

He didn't answer, but the greedy gleam in his eye as he drew close to her distracted her.

"We have no time," he said. "Perhaps that is why? And the kisses say a great deal. I had not known."

"Mmm," she croaked, not what she called an articulate answer, but his large hands cupped her face and his mouth slid against hers again in the first kiss he had initiated.

Probably not a great idea to kiss a man who didn't want to talk to her. No, no, ohh . . . a flood of pure overwhelming lust washed away the nagging thought. Her belly swooped with anticipation.

His large hands fumbled as he pulled up her shirt.

"Oh. So many layers," he said when his fingers encountered her bra. He leaned away frowning.

Before she could talk herself out of it, she ripped off her shirt and unhooked her bra. Her breasts spilled into his waiting palms. His groan of appreciation made her squirm. She'd grown so wet and swollen, even the friction of her panties against her clit made her pulse drum.

He lightly touched her breasts, fingers circling her nipples. They tingled and hardened, almost too much sensation.

"Your skin. And these breasts," he breathed. "They are wonderful." He gazed at them, fascinated. The cool air and his warm fingers and hot gaze made her shiver and her nipples contracted until they were almost painfully hard with arousal. "Yes," he murmured as he cupped her breasts carefully as if measuring their weight and texture. "They are lovely."

Strange noises came from her throat when he put his mouth on her nipple. He teased it with his tongue then gently nibbled. Candy pushed her fingers through his hair to hold his head there, just there, where exquisite sensation purled from her breast straight to her womb.

He raised his head when she shuddered. "Does this hurt?" he murmured.

"God. No." She fumbled for his hand and brought it to her other breast. "Touch me just that way. Please."

He bent at once to taste her. His mouth sucked vigorously as his hand lightly explored the curve of her breast and her side, returning to brush the pad of his thumb over her rigid nipple.

For a man who'd never kissed or seemed not to know about a woman's breasts, he did a fine job. He suckled hard. Good instincts. How far would those instincts carry him? She moaned at the picture she'd conjured.

He pulled away at once and gave her a questioning look. How those hazel eyes could look so innocent and so lustful at the same time was a conundrum she'd ponder later. Afterward . . .

"No. Don't stop. That was, um, a sound of pleasure."

"Ahh." His mouth twisted in a slightly smug smile. "So you like it when I touch you?"

"Yes."

He leaned close to her mouth, almost touching and breathed against her lips. "And kisses?"

"Yeah, kisses."

"Yes." The soft greedy sound from his throat undid her and she reached for the back of his head to pull him close.

THREE

OLLINS DOVE INTO ANOTHER thorough, heated kiss. Their tongues touched and danced. Her sweet mouth was the most delicious thing he had ever tasted. His inflamed body demanded more. They lurched sideways and lay side by side on the couch.

Curiosity mixed with feverish need shut down the last of his agent's sense of right and wrong. He pushed his fingers under the stretchy edge of her short pants and lightly caressed her cunt lips, dragging his fingers over her moisture. She put her leg over his hip and arched her back. A small mew came from her as he stroked her. His penis ached to take her. Whatever details his mind did not know, his cock would learn by instinct. By the pure animal instinct that soared through him now.

"You are so wet." He eased his middle finger into her passage and listened to her panting breaths. His hips flexed, needing to fill her. "That's pleasure, hmmm? You like this."

"Yes, I do. Please." She whimpered and her words and sounds released a tightly coiled spring inside him. They went at each other as if they were desperate animals.

No more delicate little licks, gentle graceful touches or tentative kisses. The craving demanded he seize her. They might have been starving, the way their mouths licked, sucked and tasted. He could not stop. No doubt later he'd be sickened by the memory of his actions. Several times he almost resisted the frenzy controlling him. Then she would move against him or touch him and sensation would pull him back under the driving need.

The plump feel and weight of her breast surprised him. The tentative lick on the tip of it caused her breath to hitch and the lovely dark pink flesh to harden. Oh and a firm suck on the tantalizing nipple rewarded him with another wonderful moan. The encouraging sounds aroused him as much as the scent, taste and feel of her. He listened as he stroked the damp heat between her legs and explored her curves and smooth skin with his fingers and mouth.

Grunting, he wedged his body between her legs and circled his hard cock against her. He needed the release. But the astounding buzz of desire couldn't drown out the fact that he would not plunge his into her. He must not allow himself to reach that peculiar explosion of satisfaction.

He had already gone too far, done too much. Stop, he ordered himself.

Not just yet. He'd allow himself one moment more of exquisite pleasure. He greedily drew her rich feminine scent into his lungs.

Her body's heat wrapped around him everywhere and made him pant with unbearable craving. Her arms and legs pulled him against her breasts and belly and deeper into the cradle of her thighs. When he tried to pull away it only increased the agonizingly wonderful contact on his skin and penis. Soon he'd stop, he promised himself. And then he found her delectable mouth and lost himself in more kisses.

Candy grabbed Collins's rear, firm under the silken cloth. She urged him on, directing his twisting body. The friction would have set her underwear and his trousers on fire, except she was so damp . . .

Holy crap, she was gonna come. She had never managed to orgasm unless she was alone and had plenty of time and quiet but . . . Holy—

"God!" She pressed her face to his shoulder as the enormous, relentless orgasm rolled through and over her. She screamed against the smooth fabric. "I'm coming."

He clutched her tight and continued to rub his erection against her still-stunned pussy, causing echoes of the orgasm to flood her body. She blindly sought his mouth for more delirious open-mouthed kisses.

All at once he froze, trembling. "I cannot," he moaned. Before she could protest, he'd flung himself away from her and hauled up into a sitting position. "I must not."

She fetched herself back from her melted puddle state and managed to sit up. "Oh."

Disappointment stung her, but only for a moment. When she saw the hunger simmering in Collins's eyes, she realized he fought the same powerful lust that drove her. Maybe he was too much the gentleman to take her right away. Or maybe some strange philosophy held him in check. In any case, what a lovely treat he had given her. Sure, it had only been fifteen minutes of necking, but the most explosive incredible necking she'd ever experienced. Five-star necking. Better-than-any-naked-and-sweaty-boinking-she'd-ever-experienced necking.

"Ah. I can help." She indicated the enormous erection that rose from his lap.

He drew away and rolled sideways to face her. "You have done so much for me already," he said softly. "Now I think I understand the point."

"Yeah, but you still have a pretty outstanding point there your-self." Yech. When she turned into the aggressive pursuer, she went all the way, even to the horrible off-colored jokes.

He glared down at his cock. "It will go away soon. I hope."

She slipped off the couch onto the carpet. On her knees, she slid over to him, pushing his solid, muscular thighs gently apart so she could insert herself between them. When she reached for his peculiar trousers to pull them down, he firmly put a hand over himself. "No."

"Okay," she said neutrally.

But she wasn't going to play fair. She sidled closer, put her face against his thigh, then moved up and nudged his hand away with her nose and leaned in to put her mouth over the shape of his impressive erection. She breathed warmth against him.

"Oh," he groaned. "No. No. Oh."

She glanced up into his miserable, pleading eyes. Miserable about what? Pleading for what? "Don't you like it? When you touched me, it was wonderful."

She stroked her fingers lightly over the iron cock beneath the slippery fabric and felt him jolt at her touch. He groaned and she stroked him again, more firmly this time.

"Such a lovely cock," she murmured. She could see the shape of the head through the fabric and circled her fingers along the solid shape.

"Candy," he whispered.

Unable to resist, she leaned forward to put her mouth on him again.

Suddenly he rested his hands on her shoulders. Whoa, the man was strong. He didn't shove her but she could no more move against his grip than she could push past a brick wall.

He breathed quickly and his cheeks flushed with arousal—for her, of all people.

She couldn't help her smirk of pleasure at the thought and said, "But I want to see you come."

He looked puzzled.

"Come means have an orgasm . . . um . . . reach sexual satisfaction." The word made her insides twist with anticipation at seeing that magnificent cock erupt in her hands and mouth. She wanted to see his face dazed and helpless with ecstasy. Imagining his orgasm brought her close to howling. His presence unearthed another new urge—she'd never particularly thought of herself as a voyeur. "Damn, I'd love to watch."

"I did not know that this coming was an obligation on my part. I apologize if I led you to believe I—If I . . . what is the expression? Led you on."

The rigid control in his voice brought her back to Earth with a thud, although the thrum of pure lust only abated slightly. She flushed. Had she misread his cues so badly? Maybe he wasn't as overcome with lust as she'd thought? "Of course it's not an obligation. And no one led anyone on. You do not have a thing to apologize for, Collins. You are such a funny person." Candy sat back on her heels confused and disappointed. At least now she knew how some of her former boyfriends had felt. "I don't know if you're kidding or not."

He clearly wasn't stupid or crazy—though come to think of it she might be stupid or crazy for being so convinced about that.

She got to her feet and dusted off her knees to demonstrate she was done harassing him. No way would she give into the intimations of embarrassment she felt in the pit of her stomach. She reassured herself. Hell no, she hadn't just acted like a sex fiend. He'd wanted her.

She reached for her shirt and pulled it on, sucking in air as the soft cotton brushed over the tips of her still damp, sensitized breasts.

When he stood, she at once looked for the erection. Good, his thick penis still stood stiff and ready. Ripples of major desire rolled over her.

"You need to wear something under those trousers if you're going to sport hard-ons like that," she muttered.

"I do not usually suffer from this problem. I was not prepared, not properly dressed."

"Oh, that explains it. Those are pajamas or something?"

He nodded. "Or something."

She stared, partly to admire the obvious giant erection but also curious about the fabric that covered it.

"Are those clothes silk? They're wonderful."

He shrugged his impressive shoulders. "I do not know."

He sighed and put his hands on his hips, while he glared down at the still-huge hard-on. "It should go away if you were not here, I think."

She laughed. "Thank you, I think."

He grinned at her. Such an incredible smile that her breath caught.

His smile faded and he said, "But I must go. My head is much better."

"It is," she said. "Wow, you must have fast healing skin or something."

He pressed his lips tight when she tried to come closer to look at the cut. He even backed away from her. "Thank you for taking care of me," he said. "I will always deeply appreciate what you have done for me."

"Other than waking you up while you tried to sleep, I didn't do anything for you. The rest of it was for me." Her heart sank when she realized he was really leaving. She improvised. "Would you like a bite to eat before you go?"

"Oh. Nutrition. I forgot. I must eat, of course. I came away so quickly without—" He broke off.

She considered revising the idea that he wasn't stupid.

"Well, come on," she said briskly, hiding her disappointment that he would leave so soon even though he wanted her. She led him into the kitchenette, ignoring the prickles down her back caused by his hot gaze caressing her ass as she walked. "We'll find something for you."

They sat at the counter. He ate a ham and cheese sandwich, pulling it into bits and thoroughly chewing each tiny piece. At last he opened the sandwich and peeled away the remaining ham. "This is meat, isn't it? The flavor is very strong."

She held back her laughter. Was he rude or extremely polite? "Yeah, don't feel like you have to eat it if you don't want to."

He gingerly fished out the ham and put it on the edge of the plate. He gave her a relieved smile, although he still picked at the remaining whole wheat and cheese as if he didn't know how to eat properly.

He watched her as he ate, staring at her face or at her breasts loose under her shirt, with the nipples perked into what might be a permanent happy state of arousal.

She ate a yogurt, distracted by the sight of him shredding his sandwich with those amazing fingers. The same long fingers that had touched her. Another wave of pure greed rolled over her and a strangled sound escaped her.

The glow entered his eyes. "Yes, it is very powerful, isn't it? This desire."

"You're an observant dude aren't you?" She tried to sound mocking.

"Am I wrong?" he asked, but with a lazy assurance that told her he wasn't buying any lies on her part.

"Nope. You're right. It's strong, all right," she said at last. She bit her lower lip as she gathered her thoughts. "I wonder if it's because you're a blank slate to me, you know? No history. Maybe that's why I came on to you and why it was so amazing. No wonder some people like one-night stands."

He drank another whole glass of water and sighed happily. He seemed passionately fond of water. "You mean you do not do this kissing and so on with many other men?"

She would have been insulted but she didn't think he meant to sound like a jerk.

"No, despite appearances to the contrary, I am not a slut," she said, evenly. "I have only been with two men my entire life. Other than you. And I went steady for a long time with each of them before we went to bed together." And she certainly hadn't been the aggressor in either case.

"Interesting," he said. "May I ask why did you allow me to kiss you?"

She laughed. "How soon they forget. I kissed you, Collins. I practically assaulted you. That's what I'm trying to figure out. And I have no idea why. There is the fact that I'm . . . feeling weird lately. Plus you're physically the most amazing specimen of a man I've ever seen."

His eyes widened in obvious alarm. "I am surely average."

And this was the man she swore worshiped his mirror? "Maybe you're average where you come from. Not around here. I'm average."

She looked down at her own rather plump body.

"Oh, no, you are not," he said with soft conviction. "You cannot be. I have never seen a more appealing female. I expect I never shall again."

She gawked at him and he stared steadily back. He honestly believed it.

Holy crap. Her heart flipped around a few times. What a wonderful thing to hear. She wished she'd recorded it so she could replay it a few times every day.

Her smile must have scared him again, for he stood so rapidly the kitchen stool stuttered across the floor. "Thank you for the food."

He strode quickly to the door almost as if he was running away from the attraction sizzling the air between them again. She didn't even get a chance to admire his front and see if he'd lost all traces of his erection.

He didn't leave at once, but stopped with his hand on the doorknob. "I will go now. I wish you the best, Candy. Sweet Candy."

She went to him and this time he reached for her and folded her into his arms for a long kiss, a wonderful clean flavor she already identified as the taste of him.

When the door closed behind him, she collapsed like a deflating balloon onto the couch and wrapped herself up in the blanket that she'd draped over him.

He didn't even leave his scent behind. The only evidence that Collins had passed through her life was the still-heavy sensation and the tingling filling her belly and breasts.

After a few minutes, she got up and opened the curtains. A pre-dawn gray colored the skies. Where would he go? She wished she had pushed for more . . . information at least. Like what was the man's first name? Maybe he was one of those unfortunates who had the same name twice.

He was such an odd mixture of strong, competent and something like naïve. As if he'd just stepped off the boat from some country that didn't get television. Or he'd just been set free from an all-male loony bin. He'd been fascinated by her breasts.

What kind of adult male—especially a gorgeous one—had never even kissed before?

The puzzle of Collins stayed with her through the whole day. The lack of sleep and distraction of the man made her nearly useless at work. And something more hummed through her.

Arousal. That was the word. The man had aroused her. Sure she'd had a nice earth-shaking orgasm, but she wanted more. Her whole body clamored to go find more of *that*. Please. Now.

On the plus side, the stale vending machine pastry she ate for lunch tasted glorious because her body was wide awake and ready for pleasure.

Otherwise it didn't strike her as entirely wonderful news. How on Earth could she settle for less than Collins for the rest of her life?

"CANDY? HONEY? I SAW Sammy today and he asked me when you're going to come home. I said I—"

Candy picked up the phone. "Hi, Mom."

"Honey! Nice of you to finally talk to me. But like I was saying—"

"No. I really, really know it's not going to happen, Mom. With Sam and me."

"Oh? And how's that?"

"I met someone else. That's how."

She should have used that story ages ago. Maybe she could actually convince her mother that Candy and Sam were not going to wed. Now if only Candy could talk to Sam alone and explain.

But then, as she should have expected, Mom wasn't going to be so easy after all.

"When will we meet this young man?"

Never, and, *I don't even know his full name,* and, *It was just glorious, fast attraction with some glorious, fantastic near-sex . . .* These were not going to work as answers to that question.

"Soon," Candy promised.

"How about this weekend?"

"We're not . . . Well, it's too soon, Mom."

"How about you come along home for the weekend. Wait a sec." Her mother must have put her hand over the phone because Candy could hear shouting. "This weekend is fine, Bill. You know it is. You're talking about next weekend."

As her mother argued with her father, Candy indulged in a fantasy about finding Collins and dragging him to her parents' house. How would her peculiar lover have held up against their barrage of questions? The word lover distracted her. She mouthed it and smiled.

But honestly. Would he stare at her parents as if they were fascinating but exotic creatures, the way he had with her? And the little pause before he spoke with that strange accent as if he considered a terribly important matter instead of just responding to a pleasantry about the weather.

She should go home. Now that she understood herself better, she had to explain to Sam that she needed more and that she would inevitably make him unhappy if she'd settled for less. She'd said such things to him before, but never with much conviction, because she hadn't been certain about her needs.

Five minutes with Collins had convinced her. He was the man who made her toes curl when they kissed. Hell, her toes curled now at the memory of that first tentative soft kiss. The memory of the more intense practiced kisses was enough to make her knees buckle and belly twist.

The simple taste of him had slammed into her and showed her that passion was not only possible, she craved it. Every fiber of her body and every—

"Well never mind, hon," her mother, still on high volume, bellowed into the mouthpiece. "You just come home. With or without this Mr. Right."

"Yes, Mom." She'd at last have the conviction to convince Sam they had no future. But could she get her mother off her case? Maybe she could go back to plan A.

Hire someone. Her friend Kurt was always up for extra money—but he'd probably want to bring his boyfriend along.

She grabbed her keys. Maybe it was time to finally get that drink.

FOUR

RIGHT HOUR. RIGHT DATE. The location was correct. He'd memorized maps from this time period as part of his training.

Everything lay ready. He had even fashioned a weapon out of a fallen branch. The primary historical evidence from the era—taken from a newspaper—had said that the mysterious passerby had beaten off the attackers with a baseball bat or something. He'd studied the records of the wooden bats. The object he swung experimentally certainly counted as "something."

Collins sat down on the ground. The material of his uniform protected him from the wet, cold earth. It was supposed to protect him from heat too, but he'd felt the woman's heat. It wasn't just an illusion. When he'd pressed against her body, and she'd put her mouth on him, her warmth had penetrated the cloth and touched his skin.

Gah, he tingled with the rush of arousal. Again. Just the image of the woman excited him. No, she had a name. Candy. The old-fashioned sweet food. The illegal substance that had proved to him how unready he was for this assignment.

Every time he thought of the woman and her body, he grew

hot with unquenched arousal and with revulsion at himself. He'd had years of training—the DHU screened future agents very carefully from the best prospective children and raised them to be the hope of the past and future.

A few hours with an indigenous, and he'd forgotten all about service to mankind. Rules, regulations—vital ones—had flown from his mind, lost in the beauty of the rounded female.

He imagined ripping off her clothes and then his. How amazing it would feel to hold her lush naked body against his. His fellow agent trainees frequently walked around without clothes, but their skin had never seemed more than something covering their muscles and organs. No glint of sensual power to those chemically suppressed bodies.

He was a little hazy on what would happen after he and Candy stripped naked. He hadn't gotten that part of the training yet, but he had seen naked female agents and knew that the potential sexual zone of entry lay between their legs. A tantalizing patch of hair marked Candy's female genitalia—he'd seen the curls and felt them through the tiny pair of underwear she wore. Sexual zone. Her whole body was a sexual zone as far as he could discern. He wanted to touch and taste every inch of her.

As he'd walked through the sleeping city that early morning, he'd examined the other females. Many women had Candy's lovely curves, but none of those bodies made his cock swell. He craved her with a kind of hunger he'd never imagined existed.

Hoy, his brain was inflamed again! Or rather another part of him was. He must force himself to concentrate—an easy task before he'd gone off suppressants and had been thrown into the past that contained tantalizing creatures like Candy. Hard to imagine that he'd been dubbed the best trainee of his team.

He crouched in the undergrowth near the path, occasionally

flexing the muscles of his arms and legs in such a manner that only someone standing right next to him would see his movements. Agents learned to stay motionless on their assignments.

Stifling a yawn, he glanced at the clunky object on his wrist. Approximately ten minutes.

He'd managed to lift a watch from a man while they stood at a streetlight waiting for the walk symbol. Collins had trained to pick pockets—he'd been told one of his assignments would require the skill.

He'd have to bring the thing into the future upon his return. Maybe that would help his defense. No doubt he'd spend some time in prison—after what he'd done with Candy, the adjudicators would come down hard on him but his captain would defend him, knowing he'd traveled underequipped with not enough training.

His captain. The panic threatened to rise in his gullet again. Worse than the thought of prison was the thought of a vanished DHU. What had been happening in the chaos after the explosion? And even if the DHU could haul him back . . . Gah, how was he to post his return plans? He knew the location but hadn't been carrying the proper markings when he'd been blasted into the past.

Worrying struck him as a useless exercise, but he couldn't push the fear from his mind. What if he was truly stranded? He knew only enough about this time period to accomplish his mission. How to work, how to live, how to conduct himself in a twenty-first century culture—none of that had been included in his training because he should have been here only days. Not weeks. Or months. Or more . . .

The enormity of his situation pressed like a stone on his chest. His life had always been regulated and reliable. Not like the chaos he'd experienced from the moment the explosion had occurred at the agency. Gah, he'd been trained for that sort of chaos. But he had no idea how to quell the wild lust and erratic emotion.

The picture of the irresistible Candy came to him again. He could not allow his thoughts to dwell on her. He'd demonstrated his failure in every rash kiss and touch he'd shared with her. He never should have let himself go so far.

He checked the watch that he'd coordinated to other time-pieces around the city. Eight minutes or thereabouts until the moment of his assignment. He'd memorized those facts long ago in training . . .

Four.

Two.

And then he heard it . . . Rustling bushes. A high-pitched voice raised in fear. The young boy who would grow up and not be murdered today.

Two older boys held knives. They teased the little one. Prodded him with the knives. Shoved at him with their free hands.

Collins had played this scene out so often with the trainer—almost pitiful that the attackers were skinny scrawny indigents of the past and not the well-trained agents.

He tossed a rock over their heads. They turned away to follow the motion. Good enough.

With the hideous battle cry—he'd also trained for that—he raised his weapon and rushed from the bushes. Yes, right. Just as the primary material described. One attacker dropped a knife and ran.

The other larger one came toward Collins. But this must be where the saved boy's account exaggerated, for it took only a quick thwack across the wrist. The attacker screamed in pain. Collins had probably broken the wrist.

The other attacker turned and fled. No great battle that the child would later describe to police and reporters. Silly, but Collins felt slightly let down. At least the incident had occurred, the one sure thing in two days of confusion.

The little one stared at him far too long. Collins tucked his head and sprinted away, pausing only to shout his one line over his shoulder, "Pick up the knife and get going. Fast."

Three years of training for this one assignment, completed in less than one minute.

Now he only had to get home. Where the first thing—the very first thing—he'd do was go on suppressants. A vague sorrow filled him. Did he want to give up such passion? A chance to touch a woman and have a whole world open up under his hands and in his body.

It had to be the wild state talking to him now. Not reality.

THE WILD STATE MUST have also created the panic he experienced when he returned to the coordinates of his travel location.

The small grassy spot was secluded but he had no markers. No way of putting them down. He found a rock. With the tiny metal bit of the stolen watch, he chipped at the rock, putting in the date, the proper draw power of the dark matter and his request for return.

He made it for an hour into the future and then he buried the rock. Primitive but it would have to do for the marker—he knew these coordinates would remain untouched by construction. Even in his time, the park remained an open, grassy area. The stone was not what he'd hoped to plant for a marker, but it should work. Agents routinely worked with such materials.

Heart pounding, he settled on the ground to wait, the ruined watch on his thigh so he could stare at it.

What if he hadn't gouged the symbols deeply enough? He tried hard to recall what he'd learned about the end of a traveler's assignment other than the specific dates and figures for this one. The trainers had been so vague. They had told him to memorize the numbers and locations he'd need and the rest was unimportant. He was told to concentrate on the more difficult parts of his work such as the actual assignment—that ridiculously simple scene in the park.

Twenty minutes.

Two minutes.

One. He clutched the watch hard to make sure it traveled with him.

Nothing.

He remained cross-legged and barely breathing as he sat at the exact location where his return had been calculated—or would be in the far future.

Two more minutes passed. But this was far too long.

Time froze at the moment he understood that there had been a glitch. His return. Why hadn't his return taken place? Yes, he'd traveled back to this era without a formal team effort. Yet surely the DHU had sorted out the problems and would pull him forward.

Perhaps the date had been changed somehow? It was such an easy assignment. They knew the date . . . He tamped down the panic and continued to wait.

Two hours passed and his body screamed at him to move. The sun threw long shadows across the park. He stood. Because of the precise nature of travel nothing could happen on this date. Perhaps . . . he would return again the next day for the same moment.

Only that slim hope kept him from howling in despair. He refused to face the horrendous truth. He must not panic.

He wandered from the spot and found a bench overlooking a pond filled with waterfowl. Was this the bench where he'd nearly fallen on the woman? *Candy*. Where he'd landed next to *Candy* while still dazed from the strange blow and travel.

The thought of Candy made his heart lighten. He'd expected to feel horrendous guilt but time with her had been a holiday, the first of his life. An illegal, immoral holiday that broke every standard of his profession, of course, but he could not bring himself to care when he thought of her contagious smile—and her other amazing curves.

A few separate figures appeared in the distance, walking along the gravel path. He must disappear, and the sooner he left, the better.

He should get up and vanish into the woods to rest and hide while he waited the twenty-four hours. He could find some form of food. He'd had some training for survival in the woods, although his team specialized in the twenty-first century inhabited areas, so it was not a priority.

No need to panic. It had to be the damned wild state that tied him in knots and made him jumpy with fear.

He stood and stretched.

A woman's voice called out, "Collins?"

Ah. Perhaps it was time to panic after all.

FIVE

OLLINS CONSIDERED TURNING AND running but supposed that she would shout his name again and make him even more noticeable. Best to stand still and face the one indigenous he'd polluted with his presence. He crossed his arms over his chest and waited.

Her breasts bounced beneath a red striped shirt as she trotted to his side. He kept his voice neutral. "Hello, Candy. Are you well? Out for an evening walk?"

"Yeah. I'm really glad to see you." Her smile vanished. "Are you okay? You seem . . . unhappy. Do you want me to leave you alone?"

He didn't want her to feel badly but still he shocked himself by saying, "I am happy to see you. I am merely surprised to be here still."

She gave his arm a featherlight stroke and even that faint contact triggered a rush of lust. He suppressed a jolt of response.

Candy must have sensed his discomfort for she took a step away from him. "You had plans for moving on? You are a tourist then?"

"Exactly."

"Aw jeez. Too bad you're stuck here." A smile dimpled her cheek. "Come on, you can stay with me."

He must not have hidden his dismay well enough for she hooted. "You poor guy. I swear to keep my hands off you."

He surprised himself again. "But I am not so sure I could swear the same for myself."

She beamed. "I can live with that. Nope, I'm not at all sorry to hear that."

"It is a worry to me."

She put a hand on her curvy hip and studied him. "I don't understand. You said you're not in a relationship, right?"

"I can't explain."

"Figures." She rolled her eyes. "You know what's funny though? I trust you. Don't know why. But I do."

She dropped onto the bench and stared out at the ducks as if she had all the time in the world.

Huh. Perhaps he had all the time himself . . . No return. No sign of a return. Trapped in the past? He tested the thought and the core of panic did not grow larger, merely sat like a boulder inside him.

If she had said more or touched him, perhaps he might have thanked her for the invitation and walked away, but after a few moments of companionable silence, he opened his mouth and said, "Yes."

She smiled. "Yes, what?"

"Yes," he said. "I would like to come back with you if I may. Thank you for your kind invitation."

Another short interlude. No one would suffer any consequences—except Collins, upon his return.

THE ROOM HAD BEEN straightened. A familiar scent of flowers filled the air, emanating from the bathroom. Her scent. She must have showered, that decadent form of self-cleaning he'd read about. He imagined water coursing over her naked body. Almost at once his nuisance of a cock responded.

She had bustled off to the kitchen area, thank goodness. He sat on the couch and waited for his guilt to rise. It didn't. Instead, he settled against the cushions, filled with a sense of . . . security.

She returned and handed him a glass. "I know you like plain water."

"Thank you." How could she be so aware of his predilections when the two of them were entirely different?

When she sat next to him, her sleek, rounded thigh bared by the rise of her skirt pressed to his. She did not appear to notice but he detected how her breathing quickened. Perhaps he wasn't the only one so aware of the vibrations caused by their touch.

"Candy." He cleared his throat. The ache of desire had roughened his voice. "I am not able to do what we did before. It goes against what I . . . "

She showed no hint of impatience or judgment as she waited for him to speak.

"You and I together, is wrong," he said at last.

She pressed her lips tight. "You're engaged, then? Or saving yourself?"

He was considering an answer when she burst out, "No, wait, I bet I got it. You belong to some kind of cult. That explains the clothes. And you've taken some sort of vow of chastity?"

That was as good an excuse as any he'd be able to fabricate. He sipped the water and avoided her gaze. "Yes, that is what you might call it."

She made a rude noise. "Seems like a terrible waste. The sexiest man I've ever met is some sort of monk." She inched away from

him on the couch and flashed him a half smile. "Jeez, just don't try
to induct me, okay?"

He nodded. "I would never dream of imposing upon you."

Candy's narrowed searching eyes seemed speculative. "Do you
mind if I asked you for a favor? I'm not talking about sex."

"You may ask, but much as I would like to be of help, I doubt
that I will be able to perform any sort of service for you."

"I just want to borrow you for a weekend. We'd take a trip together. To my hometown."

"No. I cannot leave unless I go to where I belong."

"That's an odd way to put it."

"Yes, I suppose it is."

Collins offered no other explanation. Candy examined him—
the man was hard to ignore. Candy's eye candy, even if he was
turning out to be some sort of odd duck after all. She wondered if
the Moonies were still in business.

"Well if you change your mind you know where to find me,"
she said.

His gorgeous hazel eyes widened. "Do you wish me to leave,
now that you realize I will not be of service to you?"

"Do you even have anywhere to go? Other than that mysterious other place where you belong?"

He shook his head.

"Naw. You can stay as long as you need to, Collins. I trust you
and I'm not going to shove you out the door just because you
won't be my sex slave."

"Sex slave?" He looked adorably befuddled.

"A joke. Don't worry about it. Want more water? Something
to eat?"

"No, I thank you."

She rose to her feet, stretched and gave a nervous yawn tinged with too much jittery awareness. Her skin prickled under his avid examination of her body and she swore that gaze aroused her nearly as much as his touch. She must be a desperate woman after all.

She crossed her arms over her breasts. "I'm beat. That was a long night last night on the couch."

"You do not sleep there?"

"Nope. I have a bed." Even this innocent conversation turned her imagination to sex. She had a bed, a big one. Plenty of room for two. They could experiment with some interesting positions there, expand his education . . . Feeling her cheeks heat, she waved at her bedroom door and checked her watch. "Give me a half hour of rest, okay? Then we'll figure out what we can do with you. Maybe find your country's consulate or something."

He put down the glass of water and rose to his feet. "No. Perhaps I should just leave and—"

She waggled a finger in his face. "Nope. Stay put. Promise you'll stay put? You won't leave without saying good-bye?"

He nodded. Maybe he'd be a good sex slave after all, if he agreed so readily to all her commands. The thought of him on his knees before her following her directives tightened her nipples. They poked against her blouse. His gaze fixed there, pupils dilated. He still felt the pull between them as much as she did. If only they hadn't made this pact of polite celibacy. She had so many better ideas. But since she respected his beliefs, odd as they might be, she took an unsteady step toward her bedroom.

"Feel free to raid the kitchen if you're hungry." She pulled off her shoes and padded to her bedroom.

Without bothering to shut the door, she took off her jeans and slid under the covers. The late afternoon sun slanted across the bed and she wasn't very tired but she had to get away from Collins before she grabbed at him and tried to convince him into a few kisses. He didn't even want to talk to her.

Yet she could guess that his resistance to her was low—amazing to think that she'd win the battle for the kisses and perhaps for making love. Her lunchtime impulse buy of condoms lay in her bedside table drawer.

But she didn't want the poor man to wear that heartbreakingly sad expression she'd seen when she had encountered him a half hour earlier in the park. He might have been a man who'd lost everything he cared about. Somehow she knew that if she did succeed in seducing him, he'd get the lost puppy look again.

Soft noises outside her room. She listened to him prowl the apartment. Why did she not believe his claim to be a cult member? He was something else, something different. She wanted to understand him. For now, she punched her pillow and rolled on her side, determined to respect his wishes and deny her own. She delivered a stern lecture to her body and heart.

Her body ignored her and pulsed, ready, waiting for his touch. Every pump of her heart seemed to shout out. *Empty, empty. Fill me.*

Alone and restless, Collins paced around the apartment. In the kitchen he opened the box containing ice—no, the icebox. The food appeared oddly raw to a trainee used to the packaged rations of his unit. This was almost like seeing the vegetable in the earth in which they grew during this era.

He walked, trying to shake off the unpleasant realization that he'd been abandoned by the agency. It had been the only existence he'd known for twenty years. Adrift in the past. The fear mingled with frustration and anger.

He stopped in the doorway of Candy's room. Her glossy dark

hair fell across her face. He'd thought hair would be messy but hers was glorious. Normally suppressed by the *clophim* his body would be hairless. Now it had grown to nearly an inch on his head. The fur and hair reminded him of animals—of the wild state.

What would become of him if he remained trapped in the past? He'd be a hermit. No forbidden contact with other humans lest he upset this era. Yet even now he yearned for intimacy with a hunger he barely understood. More than just his penis craved release. Every millimeter of his skin prickled with desire. The ache for her extended to his fingertips.

Candy. Just once he wanted to see her body and feel her satin heat. No matter what happened, he'd remember a few delicious moments with her.

Collins could walk silently—any agent could. He went into the room and squatted by the bed so he could memorize her sleeping features. If he ever managed to get home, he'd lose the strong desire but he didn't think he'd lose the appreciation for her open, easy nature.

Her leg dangled off the bed. Like the rest of her it was beautifully shaped. Rounded but not excessive. He could see the muscles under the smooth skin.

His avid gaze followed the contour of her body. When he reached her face, her eyes were open, watching him. She woke as quietly as any agent, if she'd actually been asleep.

He smoothed back the strands of hair on her face and basked in her smile.

Just like that he gave up, again, and leaned toward her. Thinking had done him no good. He would enter this new world of feeling again.

Their breath mingled as they moved close to a kiss. She

stopped for a second. "Are you sure? I refuse to feel bad about this, you know."

He might as well tell the truth. "I am no longer sure of anything about my life, Candy, except how much I want to touch you. Just once with you before I leave here. Might I ask you to remove the rest of your clothing?"

SIX

ANDY SAT UP AT once. "I'll take off my clothes if you take off yours."

He wouldn't let her touch his strange outfit but backed away and stood in a dark corner to undress. A faint rustle and the trousers and shirt slipped off of him. He carefully pushed them into the corner.

She was going to tell him he didn't need to worry, she wouldn't go through his pockets but the sight of him naked stole her voice.

He did not sport the physique of a bodybuilder but he had muscles. She'd never been attracted to overdeveloped men—she'd thought the whole bodybuilding scene was sort of silly. Whoa, that smooth golden body was about as perfect as any pinup—and silly was not the word that came to her mind.

"Wow," she murmured when she remembered to breathe.

"You are still wearing your clothes," he pointed out.

Yeah, and she had no desire to strip down in front of Mr. Perfect and show off her belly. It wasn't huge though there was a definite little pot happening there. "Oh, I'll just stay here under the . . . Hey—" She squeaked as he relentlessly twitched away the covers.

He might have been inexperienced but he was certainly not shy, and he was as comfortable in his naked skin as he'd been in clothes.

On his hands and knees, he leaned over her. "Will you take off the rest of your clothing, or shall I?"

For a moment fear sizzled through her. Yup, as she'd suspected, that was the largest, scariest erect cock she'd ever seen. And who the hell was he? For a moment, fear sizzled through her. He was so large and strong. He could easily do whatever he wanted to her, whether she wanted him to or not. Maybe this wasn't such a good idea.

He pushed back to a crouch and his hungry expression gentled. "Have I frightened you?"

"Um. Well." She sat up and shoved her pillows behind her so she could easily look him in the face. "I'm feeling a little . . . intimidated."

"Shall I put my clothes on again?" His voice was hoarse but tender.

That settled the matter. She scrambled up and yanked off her shirt, bra and panties.

If she concentrated on his glorious body, she wouldn't have to notice her own. Except now his keen pale eyes examined her with a fierce concentrated appetite. Oh, my. Only way to get past her self-consciousness would be to make sure she got so close to him he wouldn't be able to watch her like that.

Ignoring the cool air that brushed her skin, she crawled across the bed toward him. He didn't move . . . amazing he could hold steady in that straight-backed crouch, a natural position for him.

She tentatively stroked her hands over his solid thighs. God, she wanted this—wanted him—so much it almost scared her. He reached for her first. Thought evaporated. Sensation swooped in.

When his hands slipped over her breasts, all the frustration of their unfinished interlude swamped her. The wild urgency, the yearning to be filled. She might have been an animal, swollen and in heat, frantically ready to rut.

After some deep delicious kisses, he coaxed her onto her back and fondled her breasts, waist, thighs and between her legs to the wet slit of her pussy as if he were a sculptor and she was clay.

"What are you doing?" she breathed.

"Memorizing your shape."

"Come here," she demanded, reaching for his shoulders, and when that didn't budge him, pulling at his muscular upper arms.

He leaned over and kissed her stomach, his tongue dipping into her belly button. "Soon."

Now his mouth rubbed over her, licking and kissing her tingling skin. No more hesitation in him.

He pushed open her legs and snuffled the curls before licking the tender inside of her thighs, his warm tongue deliberately worked along her hyper-aware skin until it hit her clitoris.

"Ah!" She arched up spasmodically.

"Is that painful?" He raised his head and smiled up at her. His hands still gripped her legs so she could not move. Open to the cool air and his warm mouth.

He dipped down for another delicate lick. "It tastes very good."

"No. Hell no it doesn't hurt but I want you to kiss me."

"That's what I'm doing. Remember? You showed me kisses don't just have to be on the mouth." He bent his head again.

She had? Was he kidding? Oh, holy—did she care? She shifted impatiently as his tongue found her clit. Her body rose up clamoring for more. He pressed a hand to her belly to hold her still as he eagerly licked. The warm sweet pressure had already built inside her. She put her hands on his solid shoulders, needing to touch some part of him.

His hair. Soft lovely hair. She whimpered as his tongue circled and lapped her and his large finger traced her slit.

She arched up and he gave a strangled growl. "I will put my finger inside you."

She gave something between a sigh and laughter. "God, I might kill you if you don't put something there."

He slid down a few inches so he could watch with fascinated concentration as he pushed a finger slowly into her eager cunt.

She held back a shout of impatience—she wanted more, harder, now. Her body hungrily pulled at his finger.

His eyes fluttered shut. "Oh. I did not know it would be so tight and hot," he groaned.

He sounded so amazed. At that moment she understood she truly was his first woman. Incredible—and wildly exciting. The touch of his warm breath on her gave way to his tongue again, while his finger explored inside her. She squirmed, close to exploding. And he was so careful and ceremonial. She couldn't stand another moment. She wanted hot, mindless sex. Now.

She gripped his shoulders.

"Collins. Come on. Lie down."

He obediently drew away, and rolled flat on his back, arms and legs spread wide.

She sat up to rummage through her stupid drawer. Damn, damn, *damn*, where *were* they? She needed him inside her. As soon as possible. Or maybe she should let him lick her some more? No, she found the package and ripped at it with her teeth.

He'd moved to put his hands behind his head and now lay

motionless watching her. Only the enormous erection, his mouth parted as he panted and the hunger in his eyes told her that he wasn't relaxed.

She pulled out the condom. She'd have to sheathe him—she figured he wouldn't know the procedure.

Sure enough . . . "What are you doing?" he asked as she shuffled across the bed to him.

She paused. Could he be that clueless? "A condom."

"Ah, of course. I have— Oh." He reared up and his eyes squeezed shut as her hand clutched his cock.

Ah, it was good to see that clear sign of full-out lust in him. She changed her mind and put the condom on the bed. She'd make him beg first.

She could only fit the head of his cock in her mouth. Her hands gripped his shaft and slipped over him in rhythm with her urgent sucking.

He laced his fingers through her hair as she licked and sucked him, tasted his pre-come. Her belly grew heavy with the pleasure of his growing excitement.

"Oh yes," he growled. "Candy. Candy. Please."

He spasmodically arched his back and pushed up, nearly choking her. She pulled off and smirked at him. *Very good.*

"Please what?" she asked.

"I need you."

She blew on his damp hard flesh. He gave a low moan and his hands spasmed in her hair.

"What do you want me to do? Do you know the word?"

He growled. "No. No. I don't know what you call the sexual zone. But I want it. Let me inside you. I need that tight place in you."

Good enough.

She had never put a condom on a man before and his impatience didn't make it easy for her. She awkwardly rolled the rubber over him as he bucked into her hand.

She got on her hands and knees, straddling his waist and looming over him for a change. He grabbed her hips and pulled her down against him before she could hold him in the right spot to impale her. The delicious heat and the hardness of his chest touching her belly and sensitive nipples made her shudder and writhe, getting as close to that mouthwatering body as she possibly could. Against his lower belly, his cock chafed her swollen pussy lips, driving her close to the edge of exploding.

She teetered on the brink of an orgasm already. She had to have him inside her right now or she'd scream. Immediately.

She sat up and he muttered a wordless protest and grabbed at her.

"More," she explained. She rose onto her hands and knees and gripped his cock to position it at her opening.

Their gazes locked as she slowly sank onto the largest, hardest penis she'd ever encountered. A few inches down. The large, blunt head stretched her inner walls with delicious pressure. He growled low in his throat, an animal noise.

She gave a small cry as he bucked up. And then he shoved all the way into her. She gasped as he thrust so far up, she wondered if he'd hit a lung.

She sucked in a sharp inhalation. "Wait." She was stretched almost too tight.

He immediately dropped to the bed and went still, only a faint quiver through his body showing how much it cost to hold back.

She stretched out on top of him for a moment and wiggled to adjust her unaccustomed body to the marvelous swelling ache buried deep inside her.

His breath hitched with each small shift yet he didn't move.

Ready. Oh yes now more than ready. She tucked her knees along his sides so she could rise and sink, rub and slide—but after a few minutes of careful slow fucking, his stillness ceased. He took over. Grabbing her ass, he held her steady as he thrust high into her.

Collins was a quick student. He moaned and drove into her faster. Lunging—but now she eagerly could take his full pounding thumping into her entirely slick pussy.

She was so close as she rode the exquisite slide and thick heat at her center. "Please. Don't. Come," she moaned.

"No?" He panted and slowed. "No. But you. Must."

His fingers kneaded her backside even as the rhythm of his firm thrusts forced her farther up and out of control. She rested her hands on his shoulders to steady herself. Somehow he'd pushed his head up and licked and sucked her nipple. The man had raw talent.

He plunged and the sensation impossibly grew even more perfect. Oh, very. Yes. The scrape of him inside her. She reached between them to feel his width and allowed her fingers to brush her clit. At once she launched helplessly into an orgasm that seized her entire body down to her curling toes.

He drew her face down to his for a kiss, swallowing her shout of surprised joy.

They might have been lovers for years for he seemed to know how to prolong her ecstasy with very clever twists of the hips.

"Now I will," he whispered harshly.

She could only whimper as luscious echoes rippled through her. He clutched her hips so that he could thrust high into her. She wondered if her wholly sensitized body could stand the almost too intense pressure of the pleasure growing again. Joy flooded her body—as it grabbed her, her body seized at him, pulsed around the cock that filled her. A surprised shout burst from her. In answer he groaned and buried himself up to the balls inside her, shuddered and then did not move.

For several long minutes they lay together, still joined, panting. At last he murmured, "Thank you," and rolled onto his side, keeping his cock inside and pulling her easily along with him.

She inhaled a deep breath of contentment. This was definitely the best decision she'd made all day. He wrapped his arms around her to hold her close.

She licked his broad warm chest, tasting the light sheen of perspiration. "You must take off the condom," she said. "Before you, er, shrink back to normal."

"Eh." He loosened his hold to pull back and grin at her. "But I am not, er, shrinking."

She snorted at his slight mockery of her and squirmed again. This time he let her slide away.

"Oh. Shit," she said. He was right—he still sported an impressive erection. But she cursed for another reason. The condom had a rip in it. "Uh oh." She pointed and he looked down.

"I do not have any of these diseases that I know you worry about," he said mildly.

"Me neither. There's also the little matter of birth control."

"Birth . . . Oh." His eyes widened and she realized he was thoroughly stunned, as if the thought had never occurred to him. "Babies."

She touched the end of his nose. "Bingo. Babies."

His magnificent brow furrowed. "Yes, I am not taking any preventative."

For a moment, her worry dissolved into amusement—he never ceased to amaze and amuse her. "Of course not, Collins. You're a guy. There's no such thing."

He opened his mouth but apparently changed his mind. "Excuse me," he said at last and went into the bathroom.

While he was gone, she counted on her fingers. She had to be safe. No problem, she was almost certain. No flipping way she would allow herself to be impregnated by the one and only one-night stand of her life.

Nope. She drew in a calming breath for a count of ten. Her mother often talked about how hard it had been to conceive Candy. She shared her mother's genes—even if it was the right time of the month, she'd be safe.

When Collins came back, he sat heavily on the edge of the bed and leaned a shoulder against the wall. "I should never have allowed such a thing to happen."

"What? The torn condom? Act of God." She shrugged. "No regrets, remember?"

He nodded but his face remained pale and drawn. Those eyes reflected more than fear. She saw grim horror there.

No, not after what they'd shared. The best sex of her life. He better not look so entirely mournful. She'd forgotten to be shy of her nakedness and scooted closer to him. "Listen," she whispered. "It'll be okay. No matter what."

He shut his eyes. "I wish you were correct," he said softly. "But . . . " He shook his head. "I have broken laws."

Candy held her breath. For the first time she wished she hadn't allowed this man into her apartment. For the first time he struck her as a self-absorbed nut.

She flopped onto her back. "The universe will not come to an end because of what you do, Collins. And it was good. You know it was."

Collins checked the dread that surged through him. He recognized pain in Candy's high-pitched tone. It struck him that he had done worse than violate laws—he'd invaded her world and unsettled her.

He lay down and rolled on his side to face her. "It was far better than good." He stroked the sweet curve of her breast, trailing his fingers down to her hip. "And you are right. I should not howl now that the barn door might have closed behind the cows," he added, curling a finger around a tendril of her hair.

She began to chuckle. "Horses. And we are the ones to close it. It's 'No point closing the barn door after the horse bolts.' Or something like that."

He loved the sound of her deep laugh. So much more laughter than he'd known before. How had he lived his whole life without succulent pleasure? He drew in a deep breath and tasted the rich musky scent of their sex. His hand skimmed her satin skin. In that instant, his old existence seemed barren. "Do you know," he said suddenly, "I would likely do this again?"

She cocked her head. "More sex? Now?"

"I meant that I don't believe I could have run from you and your charm." Justification, again. But he liked the way she beamed at him.

And maybe he might wish to do more "more sex, now" after all. If she didn't mind. He ran his hands over the lovely curve of her lower back and pulled her to him. She smiled as he lightly tasted her cheeks, her eyebrows, her chin and then re-turned to her mouth to sink into a long delicious kiss. For a moment, uncertainty flitted through his mind but he firmly squashed it.

"This baby thing—such an event would surely be impossible," he murmured. "Right?"

"Yeah." She shrugged, a gesture of supreme unconcern that re-assured him. Her next words drove the subject entirely from his thoughts. "The cows and horses will have to wait." She splayed her hands over his chest.

"You have read my mind," he whispered.

She reached down and squeezed his cock. He moaned with pleasure at the way her warm hand enfolded him.

Candy laughed. "That's not the only part of you I read."

His heartbeat accelerated with anticipation. Yes. They would do this amazing thing together again. He would bury himself in another human being and every second would be ecstasy. Again.

The years of training he'd abandoned in this pursuit of Candy was of some use after all. Stamina helped in this situation, as did the discipline of concentration—the ability to push all other thoughts from his mind. He willed himself to perceive only the silk heat of Candy's sweet woman's body. Perhaps she could be beneath him this time. So exquisitely slick and open for him.

For the first time in his life he lived for pleasure. The rest of it, the consequences of the carnal crimes he'd committed with Candy, he would face soon enough.

"Mmm," she moaned under his touch, and her legs spread apart revealing her swollen pink sexual zone. He wanted to explore her slit's intriguing folds and plump nubbin, so he slid to kiss her there and tasted the sweet saltiness. He lapped his tongue into her for more.

He lifted his head. "Tell me the names. The nicknames, I mean."

"I'm your teacher?"

"Yes." He fingered the swollen part in the front. "What do you call this?"

"My clit." She gave a nervous laugh.

Interesting that she was embarrassed. Was it her body or his questions? He did not dare ask which and show his complete ignorance.

He continued to rub the clit as he licked one of the folds surrounding her center. "And this?"

She writhed. "God, I don't know. My pussy, my cunt."

Those names had not changed over the centuries.

Her body moved against his hand and he forgot about the lessons. She gave a hoarse cry. "Ah! No, don't stop."

The power he held over her body excited him even more and he grew harder. Excited by her breathy moans that told him she was close, he moved up to bury his face in her flower-scented hair.

"Do you have another condom? May I go inside you again?" he whispered into her ear, yet another lovely pink curve. He rotated his hips so his eager penis rubbed the slit between her legs. Yes, it understood where it belonged, deep inside her.

She handed him another of the foil packets. "Your turn."

She gave a breathless laugh at his dismay as he examined the rolled object inside the packet.

He grinned in response to her amusement—contagious this desire to laugh. Oh, but he also enjoyed her gasp and the way she writhed when he succeeded in sheathing himself and moved between her legs. That fire had to be even more contagious than laughter. His stomach flipped with anticipation as he nudged at her heat again.

She tilted and he thrust deep with his first push.

"Tight," he groaned. "Beautiful."

She wrapped her legs around his waist. Her hands slid up and down his back, urging him on. He found her mouth and they exchanged kisses—so much hotter than he could have imagined before his body came alive. Dangerous, unpredictable life coursing through him, inside her. He pushed into her and miraculously she accepted every ravenous inch of him. He buried himself in her again and again.

She threw back her head and her mouth opened wide.

When her head dropped close to his, he nipped and sucked at her lip. Candy. Every touch and kiss a crime. But no punishment yet. Not now.

Not yet.

The tension built.

He knew already what she wanted and he must not explode, not until he could feel her body clutching his penis deep inside her. First her shudder and then he'd let himself fly out of control.

Her legs clamped his waist and she gave a gruff little cry— she sounded less amazed than before. More of a purr of satisfied recognition.

Ah good. Her inner walls clutched tighter, throbbing, pushing him to the edge. He loosened his control and let himself fly as he thrust into her. The last time.

Now.

Even as the exquisite pulsations seized him, a sorrow invaded him as well.

He must leave, and soon.

SHE LAY IN HIS arms half asleep, her fingers caressing the side of his neck. He remained wide awake, knowing he must return to the spot at the same solar moment. The dark matter would be drawing at return rate then. He must go, to learn if he had indeed been stranded.

He kissed her gently, and she gave a happy, sleepy murmur against his mouth.

Even if the agency abandoned him, he would leave Candy before he polluted her and the past any further. He had already broken the most essential rules of the DHU—if he was trapped here, he would not break any more vows. That required he sink into anonymity. Should he leave without saying good-bye, was that best?

No, he was a breaker of rules, not a coward.

He drew back from an unhurried, deliciously drowsy kiss and whispered, "The time has come for me to leave you. I will say good-bye."

Her eyes snapped open and she scowled. "Damn. I don't know why I thought anything had changed. Okay. Fine. Go."

She pulled herself up and out of bed. Her trim yet succulent rear end swayed as she marched across the rug.

He ignored the desire to stroke her to lend comfort or maybe pull that wonderful bottom against him. He followed her to the bathroom. "I am sorry that you are angry."

She firmly shut the door but kept speaking. "I'm not angry. Okay, I am. I'm mostly pissed at myself, I guess. You never said anything different. I'm the idiot."

"No you are not an idiot. No regrets. It was good, better than good," he reminded her of their words.

From the bathroom, she gave a mirthless laugh—funny how he already could hear the subtleties of her tones despite their very different cultures. He did not mistake the bitterness in her voice as she said, "Yup. That's for sure. Don't slam the door on your way out."

"Candy." He took advantage of her absence to walk to the closet. He shook all the dirt from his uniform and donned it again. "Candy, I wish I could stay with you. I must not."

She came out of the bathroom rubbing at her eyes. Could she

have been crying? No. She gave him a lopsided grin. Half sweet, half sour. "Okay, Collins. I thought I could do a one-night stand. It turns out I'm wrong. Live and learn."

He felt slightly sick and realized the sensation might be shame. Not for breaking rules but for hurting her.

Her smile slowly vanished. "I'm gonna try not to be a jerk here, though I would like to indulge in a good screaming fit and maybe throttle you. I'm disappointed, pissed off, but for some weird reason, I don't want us to part angry. Kiss me."

He did but quickly pulled away. Her naked body, her scent and flavor called to him again. Instead of lessening his desire, mating with her had increased it. He supposed that soon there would be no resisting the primal pull to mate again. Time to leave before he gave in.

"I must go," he said helplessly. "I will miss you and think of you often."

"The door will be open for you," she whispered. She gazed up at him and laid her palms against his chest. "I will not bolt it against you, my wild crazy horse."

"Or cow," he said just to see her smile. She did. And that was almost too much. He stroked her cheek and left.

SEVEN

CANDY PULLED ON HER shorts and T-shirt and got to the living room in time to watch the door close behind Collins. Damn. No. She was not a sneaky person but this struck her as ridiculous. He couldn't even tell her where he was from? Although come to think of it, she'd never pushed to find out more about his origins. He'd stupefied her with his appearance, never mind those kisses and his touch. Now that he'd left, his presence wasn't drugging her into a sexual haze. Time to find out more about her mystery man.

She supposed he'd set off to the park again. Perhaps he was some kind of sweet-smelling street person? Yeah, not likely.

She grabbed her binoculars, ran out into the hall and jabbed impatiently at the button for the slow-moving elevator.

Once on the roof, she scanned the streets and park below. The view here was fantastic. As long as he stayed within a mile of the building, she'd be fine.

There.

She spotted him almost at once, heading to the park, walking quickly but with an easy nonchalance. No one else on the sidewalk appeared to notice him, despite the strange clothes and his gorgeous body and face.

Candy squatted on the gravel roof and steadied the binoculars by resting her elbows on her knees. Hidden briefly by the bushes, his tall figure soon emerged in the small clearing near the duck pond.

As Collins walked, another person dressed in some kind of powder-blue track suit appeared, running fast, behind him. A scream formed in her throat.

The person leaped onto his back.

Candy sprang to her feet, binoculars glued to the scene.

Her scream emerged as a gasp. Shit! She could do nothing but watch. His strength. He'd save himself.

Yes, as she watched, Collins hauled the person's hand up. A flash of metal? Omigod, the attacker—a woman—held some sort of weapon.

Collins twisted and seemed to force the attacker's hand up. The weapon touched the woman.

She vanished in a puff of pale smoke.

Candy ran to the roof door, wrenched it open and pounded down the stairs.

"No way. No more mysteries." She panted the words as she ran.

Her legs felt like lead, her body ached from making love. Was "making love" what you called it when a man you didn't know, couldn't begin to understand, fucked you?

Even as she raced to the park as fast as she could, she answered herself. Yes, that was exactly what she called it. Making love.

CHIN ATTACKED.

Collins didn't see her face though he at once recognized the weight hitting his shoulders. She fought as she had in their training classes. He knew her by the grip of her fingers on his neck and the way she grunted. Chin, who'd struck him as he'd entered the travel chamber.

She had come to arrest him.

No, the agency sent two for such work. She had to be an assassin. He'd broken too many rules already to deserve a trial.

Then he saw the weapon in her hand—an illegal matter destabe. It would rearrange all evidence of his nucleotides. The weapon of one who'd cover up her crime, not an agency weapon.

Not an assassin, a lone killer. He fought like a wild man.

Agency assassin—he might accept his fate. But some lone crazed murderer . . . he'd kill her first.

"Chin." He clamped his hand around the steely wrist moving toward his neck with the destabe. "No—you."

"Free the past," she hissed in his ear.

He understood. She'd joined the underground trying to undermine the agency. An anti-timey. Gah, of course he'd heard of such radical groups, but never encountered more than a wisp of gossip about their aims to overthrow the DHU. For a ridiculous moment he wondered if Chin were playing some sort of terrible joke on him. Not with that weapon. No one messed around with detabes unless they were serious about murder.

"Chin," he gasped. His arm shook from holding her back. Gah, the woman was strong. Murderous hatred darkened her face.

"Wait. I've been abandoned by the agency. I've tried to return." Why was he explaining himself to her?

"Bullshit," she said. "I saw Mostan . . . You're doing their business. I will stop you."

She grunted as she ripped her hand from his.

"No." The horrible black glow at the heart of the weapon burned his eyes.

He twisted and, with an angry grunt, shoved her hand. The destabe grazed her skin.

For a moment her form flickered—then the force of the implosion knocked him to the ground.

He pushed himself up and staggered the few feet to the spot he'd marked. The ground seemed to come up at him. He caught himself before he hit hard. He sprawled, rolled over and stared up at the sky until he could breathe again. Chin failed to stop him from reaching the right coordinates. He still had time.

But what if Chin and her compatriots had succeeded—or rather would succeed in the future? He closed his eyes and waited, clutching the stupid timepiece he'd lifted from the indigenous man—only yesterday?

Huh. It occurred to him that, after the astonishing outrages he'd committed with Candy, his concern that the watch travel with him was absurd. How long would he be in jail for the crimes he'd committed with an indigenous? A lifetime, likely. He smiled. The time he'd had with Candy was worth the price he would pay. He'd do it again, even if threatened with a thousand repeated years of confinement.

But incarceration would have to wait.

The dizziness didn't envelop him. The sun shone, birds chirped, his vision remained focused—and he remained trapped in the past. No surprise.

He wasn't even truly surprised when he heard Candy's breathless voice.

"What the hell is going on? What did you do to that woman?"

He opened one eye and drank in her tousled hair and voluptuous form. "Nothing," he said, which was true enough. Chin had done it to herself. Nothing—that's Chin. Less than nothing. Molecules in another dimension. "Nothing," he repeated.

He rose to his feet, suddenly alarmed for Candy's safety. There might well be others, Chin's cohorts, who might not follow the rules of protecting natives of the past. He had to get her out of there, away from these coordinates, fast. "You said that you wished to hire me to go away for the weekend. Does your offer still stand?"

HE'D BEEN READY TO force her to leave but to his relief she agreed at once.

The car was small, smelly, cramped and noisy. And exhilarating. Candy's feet shoved at the pedals and her hands played with a stick. The wind rushed past them in her roofless vehicle. A convertible, she'd called it. But she had said little else while they'd hurriedly packed a few of her things and taken off.

He should have been glad that she remained silent but he hated it. "I would like to learn to drive one of these," he said, hoping her mask of a face would change.

"What, you're from Europe and you can't drive a stick shift?"

He didn't answer. He remembered why he should have been grateful for the silence.

"You're not from Europe, are you." It wasn't a question. She impatiently brushed a tendril of hair from her face.

"Mmm." Collins hummed a sound that didn't say yes or no and that he hoped sounded sleepy. He leaned his head back on the headrest and let the wind flow over his face. Pretending to sleep, he gave a stealthy look at the dial on the car indicating mileage. They'd gone five miles. For the moment he could relax and concentrate on his own dismal future.

He made resolutions and broke them. Discerned the correct course of action and ignored it. He'd had intercourse—all sorts of intercourse—with an indigenous and was not even sorry about any of it. In fact he relished the memory and would for the rest of his life. Unless he discovered she'd been harmed by his interference. The thought made him shiver.

Worst time travel agent in fifty years.

She pulled off the road and he opened his eyes. Ten miles lay between them and the park. If they'd shed sufficient DNA, they'd leave a path for the hunters. They should go farther.

He frowned. "Are we there already?"

She jammed the stick into neutral and glared at him. "No. We're not going any farther until you explain some things to me."

"Things?"

"Why you're in such a godawful hurry. Why we had to get out immediately. Why that woman went up in a puff of smoke. Who you are. And what the hell is going on."

He shrugged. "I don't know much more than you do."

"Bullshit. Why did that woman attack you?"

He considered the matter and gave an explanation as close to the truth as he could afford. "She was someone I knew as a student. She was angry with me. I do not know why. And I have guessed that she used a sort of magic trick? A big joke."

"No." Her lips were tight, lined with white. "No. That was not a trick. That was not a joke. She attacked you. I saw it. She wanted to kill you. Instead you—you did something to her. I can't even guess what." She turned off the engine and hugged herself. "I could tell you needed me to take you somewhere fast. And I was scared so that's why I agreed. But don't you dare tell me any more lies, Collins."

Ah, he understood her unspoken demand—that he treat her with respect.

Something inside him shifted at that moment.

He owed loyalty to the agency. But she was more than an indigent, more than a pleasurable lawless vacation from a law-abiding life. He owed her loyalty too. He'd sworn to preserve and protect the past. She was the past, present, and . . . for now, the future.

Of course he might not have a real future. The thought made his gut go cold. If only he'd had time to find out from Chin what she had done at the agency. Could she have sabotaged the future or his marker so thoroughly that he was doomed to remain back? The thought that she might have actually overthrown the agency was beyond comprehension. Easier to imagine that perhaps the agency had abandoned him.

Candy had covered her face with her hands. He gently touched her knuckles with his forefinger, and waited to speak until she dropped her hands. "Yes. You are right. She was trying to kill me. And I was afraid she has friends who would also try to kill me and perhaps do harm to you, as well."

Her mouth opened, and closed. She cleared her throat. "Christ. Now, I wish you'd stuck to the joke story." Her lips began to tremble. "Aw, hell."

He lunged from his seat and, over her objections, easily hauled her into his lap. "I will not allow anyone to harm you," he growled in her ear as he clutched her tight against him. "No one." Offering comfort did not come easily. He'd rarely received it after he'd turned eight and left his family to join the DHU. Emotion was controlled in even the youngest recruits—with medication if necessary.

Though he'd offered the words to soothe her, he immediately understood he meant every syllable. Another shift. Loyalty, that burden he'd carried since taking the agency oath, did not fade but his allegiance swayed to the woman he'd infected with his presence. The agency could take care of itself, he prayed.

She pulled out a piece of paper from her bag and blew her nose on it. Really, bodies in the wild state exhibited quite extraordinary symptoms. For instance his own eyes prickled fiercely as he buried his nose in her hair and kissed her.

By now he was accustomed to heightened sensation but new emotion roiled in him as well. No, the sensation felt securely moored—though to a single person. Candy.

"I am the cause of these troubles," he said at last allowing her to squirm free of his tight grasp. "I will do what I can to help you."

"Tell me what's going on."

"You should inform me about the task you want me to perform for you."

She rolled her eyes. "Okay. I get it. You're gonna insist on helping but you're not talking." She put the car into gear.

She squinted at him. "Let's buy you some regular clothes."

"I came away quickly," Collins said. "I do not have the proper monies to purchase anything."

For the first time since the woman in the park had vanished in a puff of smoke, Candy felt like smiling. "Why am I not surprised?"

Her curiosity raged but they had put enough miles between them and the park that her fear died down. No killers chased after them.

Hell, she felt more than mere curiosity. There was a fair chunk of apprehension—the rest of his secrets gnawed at her.

She glanced at Collins as she drove. An image of a little green space creature climbing out of his torso should have made her smile. It didn't. But she didn't believe for a moment he was anything other than human. He was mysterious, gorgeous but as vulnerable to her as she was to him. And she knew she'd find out the truth eventually. Hints of what she understood about him threatened to disturb her.

She only hoped his secrets wouldn't test her sanity.

When they'd nearly reached her hometown, she pulled off the highway and into a Wal-Mart parking lot.

He slid out of the car, dexterous as always, and stood next to her but he refused to enter the store with her. He leaned his hip against the car. "Just buy the right size."

Typical male, after all. "It's not that simple," she explained.

"I am sorry," he said, "but I cannot go into any more very public places." He straightened, held out his arms and turned a slow circle. "Might you estimate what I should wear?"

In her opinion he should wear nothing. He should be completely naked. Though that black outfit thing wasn't bad. Belly, narrow waist, great butt, broad chest and shoulders. She let her gaze wander over him and wondered how far they could go in the Wal-Mart parking lot before they'd be arrested.

"I've never bought men's clothing."

"I have confidence in you," he said.

She gave him a dirty look, trudged into the store and bought the first shirt and jeans she found. It would serve him right if the jeans were high tide waders.

She returned to the car.

"Here." She handed him the bag and pulled the convertible top up. "A little privacy for your dressing room."

He thanked her and eyed the items in the bag. Candy should have stayed outside while he got dressed, but she joined him in the car. She couldn't resist watching as he slid out of his black thing and struggled to put on the jeans.

"You take off the labels and stuff first. Here." She reached over, took the jeans. He promptly covered his lap with his silky black cloth. Damn. She'd forgotten he wore no underclothing.

She yanked off tags and studied his bare legs and any other bits of his anatomy she could catch sight of. He was even more deli-cious than her memory recalled.

"Thank you." He smiled as she handed him the jeans.

He grunted and muttered strange words under his breath that she knew were curses as he messed with the opening of his jeans. What sort of man didn't know about store tags or how to manipulate zippers? How the heck did he fasten those strange black clothes of his? She clamped down on her vivid imagination again.

"What is your plan now?" he asked as he yanked the tags off the shirt and drew it on. He narrowed his eyes at the buttons.

She wondered if he'd object to getting naked again. Yes, this confirmed her basic insanity. Strangers chasing them both and she could feel her breasts tighten at the thought of fucking this very strange stranger again. A man who frowned at buttons?

What the heck, she'd at least keep her promise to her mother and bring around the life-changing man.

"I'm going to introduce you to my parents," she began.

"No. No more people." He still worked on the buttons of the plaid shirt.

"You said you'd do what you could to help me. That'll help me."

"No."

She groaned. "Well, that's where we're headed now. My home-town. I'm visiting my parents."

"Perhaps you should finish this ride alone," he said, softly.

"What, I'll just dump you here, in Wal-Mart?"

He rubbed at his face. "Yes. Perhaps that would be best."

She twisted in her seat and glared at him. "Best for who? Me? You?"

"Both of us."

"I knew you were gonna say that. Collins, you're a fake."

"What do you mean?"

"You talk big but when the chips are down, you back out—you don't come through."

Instead of growing angry, he appeared to think about her words. "Yes, I believe you are correct. I do not follow the rules. I don't do what is right. I do what I wish. Perhaps fake is a good word for this."

Oh, great. That was no kind of an answer. She reached for the ignition and then changed her mind. She wanted to tell him to get out but knew he would simply walk away without a word. Short-term man.

Crap. She'd had enough.

"Tell me who you are. Wait—I bet it's one of those, 'I can tell you but then I'd have to kill you' things, isn't it."

"No. I would never kill *you*." He sounded shocked. But the way he said it with the emphasis on the last word told her he'd be able to kill other people. Like the woman in the park.

Her stomach dropped. "Tell me," she said in a low voice, trying to keep the fear at bay. "I'll keep your secrets. I promise. Hell, you say I might be in trouble. It's not fair to not tell me who is out to get me."

"No one is out to get you. I'm the one in trouble. You would only risk damage if you remained near me. And they are usually very good at winnowing out the bad apples."

"You're saying you're the bad apple?"

He nodded.

"What have you done?"

"I have broken so many rules." He laughed but without a trace of amusement. "Almost nothing left to break."

"So go ahead and tell me." She managed not to scream at the man—though just barely.

"Ah, that would be the worst transgression of all."

"Go wild then." She narrowed her eyes. "Might as well if you're such a bad boy."

"Going wild. Too late for that." His warm smile looked genuine.

That smile was too much. She thumped the steering wheel. "Damn it. You could at least tell me who would get hurt if you talked to me."

Collins didn't have an answer for that.

He turned his head and stared out at the trees. "Maybe only the future," he muttered. "The whole future, blasted."

Silence.

He quickly looked over at her. She shivered and he knew she'd heard him.

"Whose future?" She grabbed his hand, her chilled fingers squeezed tight. "Dammit, Collins. You're scaring me."

What could he tell her that wasn't a lie but didn't reveal the truth?

She interrupted his thoughts. "No, wait, you mean all of the future. Period."

She let go of him, twisted and leaned into the backseat where he'd dumped his uniform. Before he could stop her, she scraped her fingers over the black cloth. He considered pulling it away but the fear in her eyes told him it was too late for that.

"I knew it wasn't like anything I've felt," she whispered. "It's soft but it's like . . . Nothing."

"No," he agreed wearily. Odd that he felt no panic or fear, only a faint disgust with himself. He suspected that he'd stopped trying to hide from her.

Almost angrily, she said, "I don't believe it."

He nodded. "That's fine."

She held the top up to the light.

He didn't grab it. No point. She found an opening and ran her finger along it. Naturally she would find the perfect angle for undoing the manutabs.

She rubbed her hand up and down. Sometimes touching it right, sometimes missing. The seams opened and closed—he knew it must look like magic to her.

She hurled the uniform back at him and started the car. "I don't believe you."

"I haven't said anything," he replied, dead calm. Protesting would only make her angrier and more suspicious.

They pulled out of the parking lot. Casually, as if asking the time, she asked, "When. What part of the future?"

"Hmmm?"

She shook her head and made a derisive noise. "You're gonna deny it, aren't you? You're going to pretend you have no idea what I'm talking about. And I'm going to feel like a moron until you too go up in a puff of smoke. Or you dissolve me or something." She shot him small angry glances as they moved through traffic. "I already guessed you were some sort of spy and then I thought maybe space alien. This makes as much sense. You're from the future. Yeah. Sure. So how far ahead?"

Could this be the right course of events after all? Maybe Chin had it right and they acted as demigods? Years of agency training melted away when he met Candy and understood personal bonds between humans. Now the last shreds of training vanished.

The words were out of his mouth before he could think it through. "Three hundred years," he said. "Or thereabouts."

The car lurched and groaned over the embankment and into a shallow ditch. He reached over and twisted the wheel so that they wouldn't hit a tree. He knew how to handle emergencies. The rest of this life—he could manage nothing.

Her hands clenched the steering wheel so hard her knuckles went white. "I knew it," she said, her face far too pale.

His heart ached though he did not dare go near her. He was the cause of her troubles. This was harm he hadn't foreseen. Yet even as he wondered what he could do, she apparently recovered.

She drew in a long breath and her hands relaxed. "I think I've known for a while. The way your cut healed so fast. The weird thought came to me that maybe you were some kind of outer space guy. Damn. It's so effing bizarre. Oh man. It's weirder than-than anything . . . Except I believe it."

They sat silent as the car creaked in protest. He had to think, which meant squelching the fear that he'd hurt the past or Candy. No matter what happened, he had to leave her. At least now he could explain. "I must either go back or remain as unidentifiable as possible."

She had drawn the uniform to her face again, and her wide eyes stared at him over it. "That's the rule? You have to hide?"

"I do not suppose there are rules for me. I am past them. I went beyond them at our first kiss."

Other cars had stopped. A man yelled, "You guys okay?"

Collins twisted and shouted back, "Fine. Thank you."

"We'd best go." Collins took the uniform from her and tucked it into his pocket. "Are you able to drive?"

"Yeah." She backed up and pulled onto the road though her hands trembled on the steering wheel.

He did not ask where they were going. There was no reason to—unless she tried to drive herself back into the area of danger.

She volunteered her actions as if he had asked. "I'm going to tell my parents that I am giving a friend a ride. Don't worry, they won't get a close look at you. But see, if I don't show up, my mother might call the police or something."

He shrugged and watched her soft brown hair flutter in the breeze occasionally brushing her grim face—but she did not appear to notice the tickling strands. What had he done to Candy, who had given him her trust? Returned her gift with the burden of useless knowledge.

He knew she would not speak of his secrets. He had confidence in her. And even if he didn't, who would believe her story?

She at last pulled up in front of a small neat bungalow.

"Be right back." Without glancing in his direction, she strode into the house.

A few minutes later, an elderly couple opened the door of the house and waved to him. He raised his hand. They were probably about to walk over and get a closer look at him but Candy gave them each a fast hug and rushed past them to the car.

She started the engine again at once. Her face was no longer as drawn and anxious. "For once Mom was about ready to hurl herself at my mercy." She made her voice high-pitched. "'Sorry honey. This was the weekend we're going away after all.'"

"They are not going to be there then?"

"Yup. No need to stay the whole weekend." She leaned back in her seat and rested her hands on the top of the steering wheel. "Almost makes the trip worth it, to have Mom apologize to me."

"Where will you go?"

"They want me to stay, use the house to crash. But I told them I needed to give you a ride. I said we're in a big hurry and that you were my boyfriend."

He studied her unsmiling face. "Then I have been of help after all."

She shrugged as if reluctant to admit it. "Yeah."

"You will be safe if you wish to return to your parents' home. And I will say good-bye."

She slowed and then drove into a road with a large sign reading Holiday Inn.

"Do you want to say good-bye?" she asked.

Of course not. He didn't trust himself to speak.

When he didn't answer, she turned to him, grabbed his hand and put it on her shoulder. "Will you say good-bye to me here in the parking lot?"

His hand tightened then slipped down to gently stroke her breast and feel the nipple harden beneath the thick layers of fabric. "Soon I will."

She pulled back just enough that his hand slipped away. "Yes, I know. I understand but for some crazy reason, I want soon to come later. What about you?"

He looked around. "Is this a hotel?"

"Yup."

She knew the truth and wanted him still.

Selfish pleasure—he'd taste it for the last time. He'd toss away every inhibition as he had her. His body lurched into arousal so strong his head swam. "We will stay here."

"We?"

He nodded.

Candy's mouth went dry and her heart galloped. Anticipation or fear—she no longer knew which. Both. Not to mention she felt very conscious of the condoms she carried in her purse.

She opened the car door and went to the lobby.

After checking in, she met him at the car and they walked across the gravel lot to the room. His gaze held steady on her even after they went into the anonymous hotel room. She wandered,

poking her head into the bathroom, picking up the television re-
mote control. He blocked her path as she headed to the closet.

"I know what I want now." He wore a fierce look and it echoed
back to the moment he had loomed over her, the naked powerful
stranger in her bed.

Only now he was even more than strange. His existence in her
life went beyond fantastic into just plain bizarre.

She inched away. "What if you're my great-great-grandson or
something?"

"No," he said, calm. He cradled her chin and rubbed his thumb
over her lower lip. "I know the names of my closest ascendants.
You are not one of them."

He pulled her against him, cupping her bottom with his hands
so she couldn't escape, and kissed her hard on the mouth. "I want
you."

Candy stiffened in his arms. God, as if she hadn't had enough
misgivings when she thought he was just a regular guy. Now she
froze on the brink, uncertain.

He froze and asked, "Shall I stop?"

She shook her head. No point in denying it. Her insatiable
craving for him had only grown. On fire for the man who hadn't
been born yet.

"I warn you, there are no holds barred." He sounded calm
though she sensed an undercurrent of something else. Despera-
tion or just intense desire?

"No?" she croaked. Was he threatening her? Her pulse
jumped—but not with fear. Not entirely.

"Do you see? I am an outlaw now."

A jittery smile flickered across her face. "But you have rules.
You told me you follow rules."

"Ah, you do understand. No rules. Not anymore. You know

the truth." His pale eyes looked her up and down, then into her face. No longer tentative or questioning. This was a bold Collins. Maybe when she'd learned his secret she'd unleashed a devil.

He stripped off the clothes she'd bought at the store, then went to her and, as if she were helpless, efficiently stripped her. His natural deftness overcame any awkward unfamiliarity with fastenings.

She backed away and crawled onto the made bed. Unsure of what to do next, she lay down. She felt nervous as hell but she opened her arms. She wanted him too much. Needed to feel that strong body next to her, his thick cock driving away her uncertainty.

He came to her. Instead of kissing or stroking her, he seized her wrists and slowly, inexorably, raised them above her head. She felt stretched and vulnerable. The action lifted her breasts. He dipped his head to taste and suck her nipples, rolling them in his mouth, scraping his teeth lightly over the hard flesh. One hand held her pinned, the other explored her, sometimes skimming, sometimes chafing her skin. He gave a gloating grunt as he cupped her already drenched sex.

She instinctively tried to shift away from this new power he wielded. It was nearly frightening, and certainly not comfortable.

"Ah." He parted her legs with his knees so she lay open beneath him, unable to move. His breath came fast. "I asked you if I should stop. I don't think I can now. I want you too much, again and again," he murmured in her ear.

"You wanted to say good-bye," she whispered.

"I've changed my mind. I wish to say hello, instead." He pressed his swollen cock against her inner thigh. "Do you have any more of those rubber things?"

"In my bag."

He retrieved the condoms. Before she had time to slide from the bed he'd lain down and with one hand grabbed her wrists and pushed her arms over her head again.

"You will leave wh-when . . . Oh," she squeaked as he stroked his free hand over her belly and thighs—over her flesh that rose up to meet him. His fingers glided over her, between her legs again, making circles over her clit, and spreading her slick moisture.

He'd gone from novice to master of the craft in such a short time. She should have been proud of her student but that tickling exciting anxiety in her belly overwhelmed all other sensation. The way he wedged her open and held her hands above her head he could ram into her, do anything he wanted and she'd be powerless to stop him.

She wiggled, trying to distract herself and him—and regain some control over her body. "What are you planning on doing?"

"Enjoying myself. And you." His fingers dipped into her folds. She gasped, more than ready. He must have felt it too because his sultry grin widened. "Oh, yes, I do indeed enjoy you."

He set her hands free and sat up. Phew. She rubbed her wrists though they did not hurt. They tingled.

With very little trouble, he ripped open the condom package and sheathed himself. She tried to sit up too, but he twisted around and captured her under his large body. No weight bearing down on her but no way to escape. Heat surrounding her, smooth skin rubbing hers to a fever.

And if she fought him?

He had seized too much control over her. She'd let him do whatever he wanted. *Anything. Just keep touching me.* She bit her lip to stop herself moaning the words aloud. *Take it all.*

He didn't take her. Instead he nudged her legs apart, so she was even more open to the cool air that bathed every spot that didn't touch him. He stroked her and when she arched her back, he pressed two fingers inside her.

"I recall the word now. Fuck. Would you like to fuck, Candy?" Her moan surfaced after all. "Yes, please."

"We won't stop. Not even when you cry out. I want to hear your little scream. Now," he said in a gruff voice.

He pulled away his hand, and replaced it with his much larger cock. With one long smooth thrust, he filled her. At last.

There was no pain. She was so swollen and wet for him, she almost spun out of control at that first huge push. Excitement made her tremble. Hunger for his touch consumed her.

She wrapped her legs around his and clutched him tight, making contact with as much of his body as possible. His cock deep inside her, he moved in small hot circles that rubbed against and in her. This tiniest motion proved enough to send her rocketing again to the dark edge of a mind-numbing climax. Not there but so close.

In a frenzy, she grasped his shoulders, arching up to meet him. She released his legs, pressed her feet to the bed and surrendered to the thick pressure of his thrusts. He cupped her ass and held her still as he pumped but she wouldn't have moved anyway. She'd been paralyzed by the coming storm. Harder, deeper . . . The first waves of almost too much ecstasy hit her and he still filled her, now harder and faster.

She cried out as the waves surged through her and hardly noticed how his pumping grew more frenzied.

"Candy . . . oh. Candy." He groaned against her hair as he shuddered. For the first time she loved the sound of her name.

They clung together until at last he pulled out of her. She gave a sleepy squawk of protest.

"I must get rid of this thing," he said.

Oh right. The condom.

Her eyes fluttered shut. Today reality had shifted and she had been well and truly fucked by the man of her dreams—including her very weirdest dreams. He came back to bed and pulled her into his arms. She slept.

MINUTES OR HOURS LATER, she woke slowly and rolled across the bed. The empty bed. He had gone. She'd asked for it and had gotten what he'd promised, no more. Now that the end had come, if she had regrets, she could only blame herself.

Her heart twisted in her chest, but she fought to remain calm. Best to just get on with life. A life that could never be the same, of course. Thighs trembling from their workout, she staggered to the bathroom and took a quick shower.

She changed her mind as the water sluiced over her face and aching body—she'd blame him too. The bastard had no right to stir her like that and then leave her empty and craving more. She thought of his tentative smile. God, she'd never see that again? She held her face up to the water to wash away the tears.

Out of the shower, she grabbed a towel and started to dry herself. The doorknob rattled. She froze then clumsily wrapped herself in the towel.

Collins burst into the hotel room.

"I had heard about these." A huge grin on his face, he held a Dunkin' Donuts bag high in the air. "I hope you do not mind that I used some of your money to purchase them? I took a . . . um . . ." He paused to think for a moment. "A twenty."

Joy stunned her. She laughed with sheer relief and opened her arms. The towel dropped to her feet and, a moment later, his bag of donuts followed, falling to the floor with a squishy thud.

She reveled as her naked skin brushed against his rough clothing. Not for long, though. He had grown remarkably proficient at stripping off his clothes. He scooped her into his arms and carried her back to the bed.

They made love slowly because her well-used cunt had grown sensitive. The unhurried thrust and withdrawal of his cock gave her exquisite pleasure enhanced by the edge of pain.

Collins liked the careful press and withdrawal into her almost as much as the furious fucking. Yes. As she opened her mouth in a near silent cry of rapture, he felt his own climax gathering with each agonizingly slow and sublime push into her. She tightened her arms and legs around him. As she shifted, he could push in deeper and the waves of his release washed over him. He liked this . . . oh, so very much. He wished he had been taught the words for such bliss.

Spent, he cuddled close to Candy and placed a tender kiss on her parted lips. They lay with limbs together in a random heap. Gentle soft kisses and murmurs. Another delight to store for the silent future. Until she asked in a too-careless voice, "What's your job? I mean I get you're some sort of agent."

How did she understand that? Had he stupidly opened himself that much to her? He wouldn't be surprised—and he realized he hardly gave a damn. Still . . .

"I can't speak of it." He stroked her inner arm where his hand rested, and appreciated the shiver and sigh of her response. He leaned down to taste her delicate skin there. A part of her body he had not yet learned by heart. He must memorize every bit of her so he'd have the memory of her to keep him warm. Even suppressants wouldn't wipe away the recollection of gorgeous Candy.

She made a grumbling sound. "You can't speak of anything. What can you do?"

He nibbled her inner wrist. "I can feed you."

Another form of illegal sweetness. He got up and retrieved the bag from the floor. They sat up in bed to eat donuts—at least until she tongued a bit of sugar from the corner of her mouth and the sight of her pink tongue awoke his craving for something tastier than donuts.

"Crumbs," he murmured as he licked the front of her chest.

"I don't have any there."

"Not yet."

She gasped—his tongue lapped from her navel to her nipple as he licked powdered sugar off her skin.

But she wouldn't be distracted. "What would you do if you could have any job at all?"

He rubbed a shiny spot, a mix of saliva and sugar, near her smooth belly.

It wouldn't hurt to tell a bit of a truth about himself. "I enjoy plants, and did well in those studies," he said at last. "I might have been a botanist, perhaps?"

"Why aren't you then?"

How could he explain the mandatory selection process? How could he explain any of it? "I was called to work as an agent."

Shut it. Even that small statement was more explanation than he should have offered. He could not allow his strange but undeniable connection to Candy to pollute her any longer.

Desire wouldn't die but he could clamp it back. Weary regret replaced his contentment. Not regret for what they'd done, not yet. For what he'd miss from now on. Time to leave before she learned too much from him—gah, what if she became an object of agency interest? The horrifying thought drove him from her warm arms.

He climbed from the bed, found the clothes she'd bought for him and pulled on the shirt. "I like this clothing. Did I thank you for these things?"

"Yup. You did." Candy impatiently tossed the pillows against the headboard and propped herself on them. She watched him as she said, "Your agency is a stupid invention."

"Perhaps." He knew she wanted to get a rise from him so that he would reveal more. Indeed, he fought the urge to tell her about the 1976 incident when DHU agents saved the world from nuclear annihilation.

He might be a horrendous agent but he would never tell her these sorts of stories. He merely shrugged and pulled on the blue jeans. He'd stuffed his uniform in the back pocket. It compacted well and barely made a lump.

She rolled onto her side. "What will you do?"

"Go back to the park. Wait and see if any other of my enemies appear. If there is a way to help my agency, I will."

"And where will you stay?"

He carefully buttoned the shirt. "I shall be fine. I have met you. I have lived better and more than I had in my past or future. I will carry you here." He touched his head and chest. Wasn't the heart the seat of love in this era? "And here." He gave a wicked grin as he grabbed his crotch.

She pressed her lips together. "I wish you'd come back with me." Her voice trembled.

She risked so much with her openness—he did not hesitate to tell her. "I wish I could."

She spread her hands. "Well?"

"Until I know it is safe, I will not come near you. And then if I can come back to you, it will only be to say good-bye."

She gave a disgusted sniff. "I thought you were an outlaw."

"Yes, but I am not a traitor," he said sadly. "I'll do what I can to return to stand trial for my crimes."

Hurriedly she slid out of the bed. "Let me get dressed and we'll drive back—"

"I will find a way to return on my own," he interrupted. "I won't risk your safety again."

"You're going now?"

He nodded.

"At least keep the rest of the twenty bucks you took from my bag." She picked up the crumpled pile of notes and the donut bag and thrust them at him. Her eyes brimmed with tears. "At least take the last of the damn donuts."

He gently pushed away her hand. "I have been taught to survive. I could never repay you for the clothes and food you've provided. I don't want to take more from you."

Candy opened her arms. Thank goodness he didn't just turn and leave. She'd have to burst into tears if he didn't at least accept her good-bye and she really didn't want to cry. Not until he left and dammit, not for long after that. She wouldn't let herself.

Their good-bye kiss was long and deep. She clung to him and for a brief moment, his chilly clothes pressed her naked skin. Then he pulled away and silently kissed her forehead.

The door closed behind him.

"You've taken more than food and clothes, you rat," she acidly informed the empty space. "You took my damned heart."

EIGHT

*I*T TOOK TWO DAYS to return to the city and then Collins trudged off to the woods, where he lived for a week. Days he stayed hidden in the woods where he drank water from a stream and foraged for edible berries and leaves. At night he foraged through the urban landscape for food. For most of his waking moments he missed Candy and dreamed of her. His excellent agency-trained memory allowed him to recall her body and smile, a small consolation. Every day he emerged from his hiding place to search for signs of assassins. At the right moment of each day he went to his coordinates and marker.

In other words, he searched and waited for nothing.

He began to feel rather like the man he watched scavenge through the trash each morning, leading a life with no apparent point. Every few days Collins risked coming close to Candy's home hoping for a glimpse of her. Not so near that he would leave markers for Chin's comrades. He didn't see Candy.

Two weeks passed. The park was nearly empty in the predawn as Collins walked there to begin the day's hunt.

A tall, vaguely familiar, dark-haired man with an erect stance strode purposefully along the path.

Collins began to melt back into the shadows but then he froze. An agent, but not one employing the usual training of conceal-ment.

This one had the brisk walk of a man determined to be no-ticed. Clearly the man made a show of himself. Why would he parade like this and make himself so obvious to any other agent? He might as well wear a sign about his neck.

Collins drew closer and recognized a rather well-known senior agent. Perhaps he hunted him.

After making sure the agent held no subvert, destabe or other weapons—agency approved or illegal—Collins stepped into the path.

"Hello, traveler."

The man stopped abruptly and looked Collins up and down.

"I am no traveler." He spoke the standard reply.

"Yeah, and I'm a duck," Collins muttered, deviating from the script.

The agent's brows knit. "Sir? Excuse me?"

"You and I are travelers on the same road."

Who invented these lines? They had sounded so noble dur-ing training. Now they did not fit this era in which Collins had begun to feel comfortable. Any native overhearing them would think that they were nuts. Was that the word he'd heard Candy use?

"I travel a road for no one. Time means nothing."

"I travel for all and good. Time means all."

The last line of the asinine greeting.

The man studied Collins, convinced of his credentials. "Who-ever you are, we have no business."

"No? Can you tell me why you're here?"

Collins guessed that the man would evade the question as he

was supposed to but the agent promptly replied. "I seek the outlaw Chin."

No, this had to be more than a coincidence. The agent's assignment must have been given soon after Collins's unplanned departure. Surely the man knew him. But incredibly the agent began to walk away.

Collins trotted after him and stopped him with a touch on the shoulder. "Wait. You know I am a traveler but . . . listen . . . I am marooned even though I have set my coordinates."

The agent studied him again, this time with a cold stare. "If you know your return coordinates, then you are not stranded. This is impossible. And may I ask why are you approaching me? I am on a mission."

Yes, it was right to be so focused on a mission and no agent should interfere with another. Collins grabbed his arm anyway. "The trainer who sent me back. Her name was Mostan. Chin attacked her. Can you tell me—"

The agent shook his hand off. "Chin killed her. Stop bothering me and go see to your coordinates."

"Did Chin act alone?"

The man impatiently glanced up and down the empty path before answering, "The DHU captured her two accomplices. They confessed that only the three of them had infiltrated the agency."

"What did they say about Chin?"

"That she had traveled to find a fledgling agent who'd escaped them during the attack."

"Collins?"

The man nodded.

"But that's me."

Naturally the agent did not look surprised.

"Please, listen." Collins spoke in an urgent undertone. "I can't get back."

The agent snorted. The man had adopted some characteristics of this age after all. Even Candy couldn't have made a better noise of disparagement.

The agent said, "Nonsense."

"Let me tell you where the coordinates lie. Here, let me write it down so that when you return—"

The man shook him off. "I am on a mission. No traveler may interfere."

Collins blocked his path again. "Don't bother to hurry—your mission is pointless. I have killed Chin."

The man pursed his lips and rocked back on his heels. He looked like a disapproving trainer examining a clumsy student. "You have wasted valuable agency money and travel by acting like a flyboy. When we meet in the complex, you will owe me an explanation."

"I'll give one now. She attacked me with a destabe and I had no choice."

"Ah," said the agent, finally showing some interest in Collins's words. "A destabe. That explains the lack of any trace or markers for her, nothing left to mark. Self-defense? I suppose you will get only a light sentence."

Collins thought of Candy's dark passion-glazed eyes and smiled. "I have broken too many other rules for that."

The agent looked bored again. "Confess your sins to your captain. You must do the return on your own. I'll tell you this—there's no mission set for you." He spoke deliberately as if rubbing in how unimportant Collins was to the agency.

He might have been about to say more but uneven voices of early morning joggers on the other side of the underbrush silenced him. The traveler noiselessly slipped away.

Collins watched, bemused. Then the implications sank in.

No other assassins hunted him—agency approved or otherwise. The agent had told him as much. Better still, the world of the future was safe.

He could return to Candy and tell her the danger had passed. Ah, his heart sped up as he imagined making a proper good-bye. He wished he could ignore the dip of his stomach—after this good-bye he'd never see her again.

Of course it was necessary that he leave and the sorrow he felt at this thought was useless. Surely he could use his training to overcome the unpleasant sensation. He ran as fast as he could, hoping to leave the pain behind, knowing it was impossible. He had earned punishment after all—not prison but an absence of Candy.

Candy opened the door and he pushed past her into the apartment, only waiting until she closed the door to blurt out the news. "We're safe. There are no more people out to kill me. Nothing's wrong."

Her eyes, dark in her pale face, told him he was mistaken, even before she retorted, "Around here we say hello when we haven't seen someone for a week."

"Hello, Candy. What is the matter?"

"The stick turned blue."

"What stick?"

"I'm pregnant."

He grabbed the back of a chair. No. Such a thing could not be true. "Pregnant?"

She pressed her lips tight. "You do know that word in the future, don't you? A baby is growing in me."

"This is impossible."

Her mouth tightened. "Then I guess it's a miracle."

He had trouble drawing breath. "I have done this to you?"

"We did this together." She laughed shakily.

"An infant." He staggered back a step feeling nearly as dizzy as he'd been the day he'd traveled into the past—and Candy's life.

For a long moment Collins stared at her, frowning. Then his scowl disappeared. For the first time in two days since she'd done the test, Candy was relieved. He didn't say anything about destroying the world with the frigging impossible pregnancy. In fact his light eyes filled with awe. That had been her strongest reaction too—joy, awe and horror, all mixed together.

Though she saw nothing other than delight in his face, he didn't come to her and pull her into his arms. He turned away instead. "No. Wait. I must go at once. Now I see why the coordinates disappeared. Could that be why he showed up? Gah, it's clear!" He raced out, slamming the door behind him.

Just like that. Gone again.

Candy dropped onto the couch and considered crying but she was too annoyed with the man. She'd have to raise this baby without ever explaining who its father was?

Fat chance. She'd tell the baby and anyone who listened that Dad was some kind of traveler from the future.

And maybe the baby would come visit her in the lunatic asylum.

Okay, fine, an anonymous sperm donor was a good story and God knew he was the perfect donor. That at least cheered her a bit—it didn't erase the horrible, useless bitterness inside her.

She didn't have much time to consider the matter because within ten minutes, he reappeared, out of breath, holding a stone covered with crudely carved shapes.

"Do you have a hammer?" he asked.

Yes, and she considered taking out the hammer and beating

him with it, or at least ranting at him. Instead she pulled the small hammer from the utility drawer and handed it to him.

He put a dishcloth on the floor and put the stone on the floor on top of it. His slender strong fingers were grubby as if he'd been digging in dirt.

He paused and pointed at the cloth. "This might be ruined. Do you mind?"

She shook her head. "But what are you going to do with it?"

He dropped to his familiar crouch then folded the cloth around the rock and began to whack it with the hammer.

"The agency knows," he said as he pounded.

Not really an answer but she didn't interrupt as he went on. "They must know that you will have this baby and that I am the father. My DNA has to be everywhere. I bet even the agent I met today knows."

He paused and looked at her, a broad grin spread across his face. "Of course he does. That must be why he made himself so obvious—marching up and down, waiting for me to attack or speak."

He shifted so he rested on his heels, and started pounding again. "I'm thinking he wasn't even sent back for Chin. They would have sent two back to deal with her. Why then? Just to get the information from me or maybe to pass it along? Though I don't understand why he could not tell me I am fated to remain here."

He stopped again, the hammer loosely gripped in his hand, and scratched thoughtfully at his chin. "Perhaps because I needed to reach this answer on my own? No, the agency is not a sentimental organization. Perhaps it was a way to tell me my services were no longer needed? Maybe they knew I would come back to you and they did not want to give me too much information."

He went back to hitting the rock until it was reduced to dust. "Ah well. Too bad I'll never know why the agency must act with so much mystery." Collins didn't sound unhappy. In fact Candy could swear she heard joy in his voice.

She leaned against the wall, arms folded, watching. "You might not care about mysteries but I'm sick of them. Are you going to ever make sense? At least tell me what you are doing."

He stood and tipped the dust into the trash can. "Destroying my marker with my travel coordinates. Staying. I don't know what sort of use I shall be to you and our . . . " He wiped his hands and gazed down at her belly. "Perhaps I could become a botanist after all. Whatever I do, I will not leave you both to fend for yourselves."

Her heart bounded upward into her throat. "You won't?"

He moved close to her. He'd grown the start of a golden brown beard, which lent him a disreputable dangerous air. No more pretty boy—he was all man. He went to her and pulled her into a deep hungry kiss, tinged with something new. Possessiveness.

"You are mine," he whispered as he stroked her hair.

"Ha. That's what you think."

He backed away but kept his strong hands wrapped around her upper arms. "Was I wrong to stay back? I should have asked you first? I know I have interpreted the agent correctly. But you . . . " He spoke in a low, urgent voice. "You'll have an infant. I cannot leave when you—"

She laughed, giddy with delight. "No, no. All I meant was that you're *mine*. I'm the one who found you. *I* get to keep *you*."

He didn't so much as crack a smile. "Yes, you do. I have felt something for many days. As I came here again I knew. I understood." At last he grinned—one of those gorgeous radiant smiles that stole her breath and made her want to beg. "I have such an education with you," he said. "For example, I thoroughly comprehend the word fuck."

"That's what you thought of as you ran over here?" She prodded him hard in the ribs with her finger.

"Ah, indeed I did." The smile was wicked yet it glowed with a soft light. "I thought of all that I've learned with you. The most interesting fact you've taught me is how much I love you."

He swooped in for a longer and even greedier kiss.

"Collins. Me too," she whispered against his mouth.

Her answer set him off. He kissed her face and worked his way, with light skimming caresses of his mouth, down her neck to her breasts, his soft new beard tickling her skin. He punctuated his kisses with words.

"Keep me forever." He traced a thorough path with his tongue and lips back to her mouth. "Let me serve you instead of the blasted agency." He yanked her shirt from her waistband, and his fingers trailed up her back.

"Yes," she gasped as his large hands traced the path of her spine then pulled her firmly against his erection. "Yup. Your service can commence at any time."

WOLF IN CHEAP CLOTHING

CHARLENE TEGLIA

ONE

BLONDE WALKS INTO A bar . . .

A Louise Catrell figured it was her way of coping with anxiety when the opening of a bad joke was all she could think about as she stood just outside The Big Kahuna. But it was going to be fine. No need to get nervous. She would blend right in with the crowd of surfers and college students who frequented this beachside Southern Californian bar.

Surfer music poured out into the night and mixed with the sounds of the wind, the waves lapping at the shore and the drone of traffic on the nearby highway, all so normal that it soothed her nerves.

She glanced down at her clothes. The bikini in a bright watermelon shade that barely covered her nipples and covered even less of her ass was more than some of the women who'd gone in ahead of her wore. But even in her attempt to play Beach Slut Barbie, Lou couldn't quite bring herself to parade around like that in a risky situation. So she'd added a denim miniskirt. It bore more of a resemblance to a really wide belt that hugged her hips than a skirt, but between it and the bikini bottoms, she felt slightly more protected. Although the effect of her C-cup curves mostly exposed

struck Lou as borderline pornographic. It was almost more suggestive of a harness than a bikini top.

The white canvas sneakers instead of sandals were a calculated
risk. She didn't want to have to kick off her shoes if she needed
speed, and they suited the casual but sexy look she'd cultivated.
A denim jacket hung over her arm since the outfit didn't leave her
any place to store her wallet and car keys. She wanted to wear it
and add another layer of protection, but she was there to attract
attention, not hide from it.

Her bleached-blond hair was pulled into a bouncy ponytail
and contrasted nicely with her heavy black mascara and hot-rod
red lipstick. With any luck her appearance would do all the work
for her. Picking up a guy would be as easy as fishing with dyna-
mite. Really, it was almost cheating.

You look like a cheap slut, Lou, she encouraged herself silently. *Perfect. Now embrace your inner bimbo and go get him.*

Right. With a deep breath that threatened what little modesty
her bikini top retained, Lou straightened her shoulders, tilted her
chin up and went in.

As soon as she opened the door, the full volume of the music
hit her. She was practically going to have to shout to be heard.
Another good reason to let her clothes and her body do as much
of the talking as possible.

Fortunately, her body had plenty to say on the topic she
wanted to broadcast. There was a swing in her hips and an ease in
her stride, an earthy sensuality in her movements that came from
being a very physical creature at home in her skin. Even her scanty
outfit didn't disturb her aside from the scanty protection it offered.
Smooth bare skin was so easily damaged.

A year ago she hadn't been like this at all—relaxed and sensual
and physically alert at the same time. She'd been a tense, hurried

woman in a business suit, uncomfortable with herself and her world. Always trying to perform, to project the right tone. She hadn't enjoyed the sheer physical pleasure of being alive, feeling the sun or the wind on her skin, savoring flavors on her tongue. Well, she was very aware of the pleasures of being alive now. Nearly getting herself killed had done all kinds of things to her perspective.

Lou worked her way over to the crowded bar, angling herself sideways when she had to, sliding through dancers and people talking in groups. Once she reached the wide oak bar, it was easy to catch the bartender's eye. A quick glance told her the rest of the crowd was drinking beer and Jell-O shots. Ugh. Well, she had a cast-iron stomach. With a mental shrug, Lou indicated with a nod of her head that she'd have what everybody else was having.

Her Jell-O shot and draft beer appeared in front of her with impressive speed. This bartender was really earning his tips tonight. Either that, or she'd won him over just by standing there jiggling.

She jiggled a little more than she had to while she dug out her wallet and pulled out a bill. He deserved it for being such a nice boy.

A male hand covered hers just as she was sliding the money over the bar. "Let me buy you a drink."

It wasn't a question. He was making it a statement. Pushy. Lou knew without even looking that he wasn't the one. Still, she turned her head to see what kind of fish she'd hooked.

He was big and good-looking for now, but his habits would start showing in his face and his body within a few years and then he'd lose what little appeal he had. He wouldn't know that, however. He was sure he was God's gift to women. His kind wouldn't go away without a push, and she couldn't have him hanging around getting in the way.

A subtle push, though. She was supposed to be an easy lay, not the type to rip a man to shreds.

She let a little of her true self show in her eyes and leaned close, letting her nose nearly touch his before she answered. "You're looking for somebody else. I turn into a real bitch once a month and it's almost that time."

Nobody else who was standing nearby would see or hear anything amiss. She was smiling and keeping her body loose and relaxed. From any angle she would look anything but threatening. All the threat was in her eyes and her voice, pitched so only Mr. Wrong could hear.

He didn't take it well but he backed off. "Stupid bitch," was the best parting shot he could come up with. Lou barely kept herself from shaking her head. Really, he was so far out of his league it was pitiful.

Not like the one she'd come hunting for. That one was a predator and he would take all of her skill to handle. She'd done her best to prepare. She had the advantage of surprise. She'd stacked the odds as far in her favor as she could manage. But she didn't kid herself that it was going to be easy with him.

And then suddenly he was there. She felt him, her skin prickling with the sense that she was being watched by something dangerous, long before she saw him.

He was dressed to blend in like she was and it was just as certainly a costume. Silk Hawaiian print shirt worn open to expose a broad expanse of chest and washboard abs tanned a nice shade of golden. Denim jeans with the top button undone. Scuffed leather deck shoes over bare feet. Dark brown hair worn long enough to show the natural curl and streaked with gold from the sun. Little lines around the corners of his brown eyes that made it look like he was smiling when he wasn't. Everything about him said California beach lover, except for the eyes. They were too sharp and watchful to match the lazy, good-times pose.

Lou looked around the bar and observed the rest of the crowd with her senses on full alert, comparing and cataloging. She didn't think she was mistaken. He was the one, the wolf in the crowd of harmless sheep.

And he was going to come right to her.

She made eye contact with him and lifted her Jell-O shot in an almost salute. She tipped her head back slightly in a move that lifted her breasts and bared her neck as she put the glass to her lips and let the contents slide down her throat.

He was beside her before she settled the empty glass back down onto the bar.

"Hello."

She liked his voice instantly and wished she didn't. It had a deep, husky timbre that made her want to growl in response.

"Hello, yourself," Lou answered. Her voice was as Midwestern as his and that was the clincher. He didn't belong here either. He wasn't any more of a local than she was, but he'd been here long enough to acquire the tan. That fit. The one she'd come looking for had vanished from Michigan almost a year ago and all signs pointed to this California bar as his new hunting ground.

Up this close she could see that his eyes were more amber than brown, flecked with gold. Wolf's eyes. He smiled at her and she wanted to smile back. Since it was in character, she let herself.

"Can I buy you a real drink?"

What an opening. She took it. "Now that you mention it, I have a real craving for Sex on the Beach." She put enough jiggle in bending toward him to make a lesser man's eyes cross and enough innuendo in her voice to make her meaning clear to a man with the density of plutonium.

"Really." His smile broadened. "I think we can work something out. Do you want to finish your beer first?"

"Absolutely." There wasn't enough alcohol in either glass to endanger her. It would take a whole lot more than a couple of drinks to overpower her new metabolism, but it might take the edge off her nerves. She chugged the beer without hesitation and slid the empty glass next to the shot glass. The bartender had picked up her ten-dollar bill and placed her change on the bar already. She left it for him.

Then she curled her hand over her wolf's arm and felt the surge of something powerful and surprising spread through her from the point of contact. It took a real effort of will not to tighten her hold on him, not to lean into him and slide more of her bare skin against his to heighten the effect.

She hadn't felt anything like that before, but then, she'd changed. Lou forced herself to focus on the task at hand and let him lead her out into the warm, waiting night while The Beach Boys sang an incongruous accompaniment.

Nothing really bad ever happened in the endless summer world of The Beach Boys. Whatever happened tonight, Lou was pretty sure it was going to be bad.

When he slipped behind her and snapped handcuffs on her with inhuman speed, it confirmed the bad feeling.

TWO

"THIS IS SO SUDDEN." Lou pitched her voice seductively low to cover the waver of alarm in it. She wiggled the hands currently cuffed behind her back and went on, "Usually there's some small talk and foreplay before the handcuffs come out."

"Nothing stopping us from talking now," a lazy masculine drawl pointed out from behind her. Very close behind her. "And as for the foreplay, with handcuffs on you it means I have to do all the work."

Dammit. He was seriously going to leave her like this. Lou closed her eyes and cursed inwardly. Out loud would feel better, but it would also ruin her current persona of party girl on the prowl.

The evening was not going according to plan.

"Look. This is a little fast for me." She shifted forward, away from his body heat and his breath on her bare shoulders. "I don't usually do bondage on the first date."

"We're not dating," he pointed out. "We're not even having a one-night stand. You picked me up in there and brought me outside to have sex on the beach."

"That could take all night, if you do it right," Lou said, starting to feel annoyed. Honestly. Men. "We didn't exactly get specific in the bar. It was too noisy. I didn't say I wanted you for a five-minute quickie."

"You implied you could be easily satisfied." A hand trailed down her spine, toyed with the silky fabric of her bikini top and then slipped inside the waistband of her almost a skirt.

A hand that belonged to a total stranger. A stranger who might be a killer. And she was helpless. Shit, shit, shit.

"Seriously, you have to let me go for a minute. I need to get something from my car." Lou leaned back against him, letting her body relax into his. Strangely easy to do, given the circumstances. Something about him made her want to rub against him and luxuriate in the contact.

"And then you won't object to me putting the cuffs right back on you?"

"Hey, if it means you'll do all the work . . . " She let her voice trail off into what hopefully sounded like a sexy laugh and not hyperventilating panic.

"And what's in your car that's so important?"

A gun. Loaded. "Condoms, silly."

"I have condoms."

Just her luck, he was prepared. Or was he lying to her? "Let me see," Lou demanded. She tossed her head, a movement that made her blond ponytail tickle his bare chest. Hopefully it distracted him.

She felt his body shift, felt his hand slide into the front jeans pocket that her barely covered butt was now plastered up against and heard the crinkle of a foil-wrapped package. He reached around her bare waist to display it on his open palm. "There."

"It's too dark," she hedged. "I can't see what kind. I always use ribbed and lubricated."

"Picky." His voice was clearly amused. Well, that was something. It beat homicidal rage. "I'm in charge of foreplay, remember? Lubrication won't be a problem."

"What about the ribs?" Lou decided it was perfectly in character to harp on that point. A real party girl would demand ribbed for her pleasure.

"I think you'll find me adequate without enhancement." The hand holding the condom pressed against her belly, molding her butt more firmly against the hard ridge of his erection. Lou felt her eyes widen in surprise. Adequate? That was an understatement.

She dragged her mind away from his demonstrably adequate equipment and back to the sticking point. He wasn't going to be talked into letting her go. Which might be fine if he really didn't have anything but uncomplicated sex in mind, but there was that *if*.

"I know what you're doing."

Cold fear knifed through her belly. "W-what do you mean?"

"You're stalling." His other hand came around her waist, slid low and rubbed a slow circle over her mound, subtly stimulating her clit. The thin denim fabric of her skirt felt like an incredibly inadequate layer of protection between her flesh and his hand. "Are you afraid to submit to me and ask for my protection?"

"That's it," Lou said, latching on to his explanation. Then she realized it made no sense at all. "I mean, what?"

"You're a strange female in my territory." His breath touched her bare neck seconds before his lips did. "You're unmated. I'm the alpha. You have the right to ask for my protection and the protection of my pack if you submit to me."

"Um, I think you have the wrong girl." She shivered. His lips had no business feeling seductive and wonderful on the curve of her neck. But then a lot of serial killers were probably practiced seducers, which was how they got their victims alone and vulnerable.

Teeth closed over her neck and bit into the skin. "Ouch! Look, this has gone far enough. I've changed my mind."

He let out a low growl. It resonated over her skin and slipped underneath, making something inside her hum in response.

To Lou's disbelief, her body betrayed her. Her head fell back, exposing her throat to him. He was alpha and she was submitting to him.

Terror filled her. This was it, the nightmare she'd lived with for so many months. Teeth were going to slash and rend her exposed flesh, her blood would spill, her bones would shatter. She'd survived before, but what if he recognized her and made sure to finish the job this time?

"You taste like fear." There was a new sound in his voice. Rough, aroused, animal.

"No shit," Lou sobbed out. If she'd been able to move, she would be fighting for her life, but some insane paralysis held her captive.

"Has the alpha of your own pack hurt you, little wolf? Is that why you're afraid?"

There was something besides arousal in his voice. Anger. It fueled her panic and suddenly Lou found she could overcome the instinct to submit with the instinct for survival. In a fury of motion she used her feet, the weight of her body, the metal of the handcuffs, everything at her disposal fueled by inhuman strength and agility to fight for her freedom.

A human male would never have been able to hold her, handcuffed or not. But this was no human male. This was an alpha werewolf in his prime, and not even the extra-strength terror lent her was enough to break free.

He subdued her. He forced her to the ground, facedown, and pinned her there with the full weight of his body. She fought on, trying to break his hold, until finally all her strength was gone and nothing but defeat remained.

Lou went still underneath him then, vibrating with a mixture of fear and fury at the inadequacy of her body. Her new senses, her new strength, none of it was enough.

"I guess that's my answer." He picked up the conversation easily, as if she hadn't just done her best to maim him for life. "You're not going back to him."

No, of course she wasn't. She wasn't going anywhere, ever again. This was it.

Lou closed her eyes and waited for her life to flash in front of her. It didn't happen, which was probably just as well. The last significant event in her life was being mauled and left for dead and she really didn't want to relive it in her memories just before reliving it in the flesh.

She'd survived only because her blood contained the antigen that triggered the transformation when it mingled with the blood of the were who'd attacked her. Now that she was a were herself instead of a human female, he'd be more thorough. There'd be no miracle to save her this time.

She huddled into the sand, still warm from the sun, and waited for him to strike.

"Still with me?" His lips grazed along her neck and nipped lightly at her earlobe. "I'd feel bad about this right now, but you picked me up. If you like it rough, I'm okay with that. Rough play can be fun. But that didn't feel much like foreplay to me."

Oh, hell, he was going to get chatty first. Why didn't he just kill her and get it over with? She couldn't stand it, she really couldn't. "Don't drag it out, for heaven's sake. Just do it."

"And you wonder why I got the impression you didn't want a man who could go all night." Amusement tinged his voice. "You'd probably bitch at me later about insufficient lubrication if I just did it. Wrestling in the sand with me just now didn't get you wet?"

"Like it matters," Lou growled.

"It matters. I have a reputation to think about. And I know your type. If I don't make sure you come at least three times, you'll go back inside and tell everybody I'm lousy and probably a premature ejaculator. The men won't respect me. All the women will spread the word. And I'll never get laid in this town again."

He sounded aggrieved. He was laughing at her, the jerk.

"Didn't your mother teach you not to play with your food?" she snapped back.

That made him laugh outright. "Is that your subtle way of asking if the big, bad wolf is going to eat you?" He tugged at her ponytail and nuzzled her earlobe. "If you wanted oral with your bondage, you only had to ask."

Lou let out a strangled shriek of frustration. She was going to die and he had to pick now to play comedian.

He hadn't been nearly this good-humored in Detroit. Lou frowned and thought about that. Which was difficult, with him nuzzling and nibbling at her, toying with her barely dressed body and generally creating a world-class distraction. But she had a very practical, logical mind from years of working in health insurance claims and she forced it to sort out the facts.

It was a fact that a werewolf had nearly killed her in that alley outside a bar with a reputation for being the local meat market. She'd been passing by, heard a woman scream and run to help. Only instead of fighting off a thug like she'd expected, she'd found the woman being attacked by what looked like an enormous wolf.

While Lou watched, horrified, the wolf finished the woman off and she'd quit screaming forever. And then it had licked its bloody muzzle and launched itself at her.

After that she wasn't herself once a month and the lunar cycle took on a whole new importance in her life. She'd been attacked by a werewolf, and now she was one too.

The string of killings around the Detroit bar ended that night. Up until then, five women who'd reportedly been in the bar at some point on the evening of a full moon wound up dead. Most of them had been killed in their own cars, parked nearby.

Then a similar series of murders had happened every full moon in the vicinity of this bar for the last three months.

So the wolf she was after had to be around here somewhere. She'd gone into the bar looking for him, hoping to draw his attention by playing to his type, a harmless-looking girl in search of a good time with an available man. And unless she'd missed something, the only werewolf in the place besides herself was now massaging her hips and kissing his way along her bare shoulders. And making jokes.

There was also the fact that the animal inside her liked him with an enthusiasm never before displayed toward any other person. She'd learned that her animal self had instincts and an inner wisdom that were more reliable than human reasoning, as well as far more acute senses. Now that she thought about it, she didn't really believe her inner wolf was wrong to trust him.

It didn't add up. But he'd called himself the local alpha and mentioned his pack, like he was in charge around here.

Lou's eyes went wide. And he'd singled her out and snapped cuffs on her. Not a coincidence. If she hadn't given him an excuse to get her alone, he would have come up with one. She'd done his job for him. No wonder he was in such a good mood.

He was after the killer himself, and he probably thought he had his man. Woman. Wolf. Whatever.

"That really isn't necessary," Lou said, trying to wiggle away from his busy hands and mouth, although her heart wasn't really in it. And when he interspersed kisses with little love bites, she shuddered in response. It felt far too good. The animal side of herself wanted to get closer, wanted that strange buzz of power that spread from him to her to continue and grow.

"I think we already established that it is. Lubrication, your orgasms, my reputation?" He caught the edge of her skirt and tugged it down her legs. "Although I'm more than happy to just get right to the oral sex if you're ready for me to move on."

"Stop for a second. We need to talk."

"You know, conversations that start out with *we need to talk* never end well. Why don't you hold that thought until after you've had an orgasm or two?"

Lou's teeth ground together so hard he had to be able to hear them. "Now."

He tugged her bikini bottoms down, following the trail her skirt had blazed. "Don't worry, I won't let any sand get into sensitive places."

Since he had her hips lifted up, she was startled to notice, she wasn't in any immediate danger. And then he shrugged his shirt off and slid it underneath her as a protective barrier against grit before stroking his hands along her ass cheeks and pressing them down. "You have an amazing ass."

She closed her eyes and tried very hard not to notice what he was doing to her ass with those busy hands and lips of his, but since it felt pretty amazing, she had to give that up as hopeless. Lubrication was not going to be a problem. She could feel her sex swelling in anticipation of getting the same attention from him, growing embarrassingly wet in the process. He bit the curve of one ass cheek just hard enough to sting, licked the sting away and massaged his fingers in circles that went lower and lower until they nearly grazed her waiting cleft.

"Talk. Now," she choked out before she lost her powers of speech completely.

"All right, if you insist." He rolled her onto her side and spooned up behind her. And slid one hand between her legs from behind to cup her naked mound, sliding an expert finger around and over her clit. His palm pressed against her puffed-up cunt with a pressure that was both a welcome relief and an even more tantalizing tease. His other arm curled around her from the side. His free hand slipped inside her bikini top to roll a nipple between two fingers. "I think we need to work on the lubrication some more."

A choking sound escaped her. Oh, hell, maybe he was right. Talk was cheap, but a curl-your-toes, roll-your-eyes-back orgasm was priceless. The strange, sizzling something that spread from every point of contact with him and surged through her told her any orgasm she had with him would be a world-class mind-bender.

She wanted that orgasm. In fact, she needed it. Bad. They could straighten out the misunderstanding later.

Urging him on with her hips, Lou slipped one leg up over his to give him better access. He obligingly speared her aching pussy with one finger and then slid another one inside to keep the first company. She made a strangled sound of encouragement and when he moved his other hand down to stroke her clit, she gave up on everything but riding his hands until the promised orgasm ripped through her and drenched his fingers.

It did, in fact, curl her toes and make her eyes roll back, and when the last ripple ended, he continued to use his front hand to toy with her clit and her nipples in turns while his fingers moved inside her from behind until she found herself feeling pretty interested in having another one at his hands. So to speak.

"You have a point," he said, stroking his fingers along her slick and swollen cunt with thorough attention. "There is something I have to say before this goes any further and if I don't say it before I take my jeans off, it'll be too late because my cock is going straight inside you."

Lou's vaginal walls contracted sharply around the fingers still buried inside her at his graphic words.

"I take it you don't have a problem with that."

She should, she remembered that vaguely, but it really didn't seem important now. Especially with her muscles half relaxed from pleasure and half tensed to experience more. What seemed important was getting his wonderful cock inside her, deep inside, riding her hard and fast from behind. As good as his hands felt, she needed more. Deeper penetration. The sensation of having her needy cunt stretched and filled to capacity with his cock. And having him do it to her while she was handcuffed and helpless filled her with heat that outmatched her earlier fear.

"Fuck me," she said in response.

"Do you understand what's happening?" As he asked the question, he slid his hands free of her to strip away his jeans and Lou nearly cried out at the loss. She writhed back against him to keep some part of her in contact with him, needing the touch of his flesh against hers even more now.

"Yes. Apparently getting handcuffed by a stranger turns me on. Hurry. Get naked," she snarled back. She'd never felt this before, this fire, this building feeling inside as if some strange power had been summoned by his touch and it needed to keep building until it was big enough to do . . . something. She had no idea what, but she knew instinctively that they had to keep touching, that they'd started something that couldn't be stopped without concluding however it was meant to.

He rolled her up onto her knees and nudged them wide apart. She could feel the head of his cock, hard and ready, right where she wanted it. His hands slid under her and supported her hips since with her hands cuffed uselessly behind her she might have collapsed flat to the sand with his first thrust.

Lou waited for it, the strange, coiled thing inside her waited for it, until the sense of building power nearly choked her. His breath ruffled the hair at the back of her neck as he growled out another question. "Do you want me?"

If she hadn't been on fire with need she would have rolled her eyes. What did he need, an engraved invitation? Okay, maybe he did. Maybe he wanted to be sure there wasn't any misunderstanding here. But if she hadn't been handcuffed, she might have been tempted to slug him. The delay was unbearable. "I thought only a vampire needed verbal permission to enter," she grumbled.

He vibrated against her with laughter. "Answer the question."

"Yes," she answered, thrusting back with her hips to make the message unmistakable.

"I'd stop if I could," he told her. "I wouldn't put you in danger willingly. I give you my protection, now and always."

Lou had a hazy moment to consider the potential hazards of werewolf sex and to wonder why he could possibly want to stop. The danger posed by the rogue werewolf seemed distant and unimportant. Still, his protective streak seemed kind of nice, really. He might not ever take her on a date or make the coffee in the morning, but he delivered a one-night stand with real flair.

Then he was thrusting into her, hard and deep, and the growing, thrumming thing inside her fed on it, getting stronger with each plunging stroke of his cock into her wet and aching cunt. And it still wasn't enough. She needed more, needed him to do something else.

Lou let out a fierce, wordless sound of need and demand. He responded, making his thrusts faster, slamming into her again and again. Power flooded her body in surges, each one stronger than the last, in time to his rhythmic thrusts. Just when she felt like her skin would split, it was too big to contain, he dug his fingers into her hips hard enough to bruise and impaled her with his thick cock in one final plunge.

She could feel his cock swelling even bigger and then spurting hot liquid deep into her core and that touched off both her own orgasm and the alien energy inside her. It was like shapeshifting but not quite the same. She kept her human form but felt an unmistakable sense of transformation taking place. It shook her entire being and drove the breath from her body.

Lou jerked helplessly under him, held fast by his hands, his body and his cock, caught in the throes of an unbelievably violent orgasm and something else that started somewhere in the center of her body and shot out in all directions as the power released. She wouldn't have been surprised to hear windshields shattering from the cars parked outside the bar. It didn't seem possible that a force like that, suddenly unleashed, could go unnoticed.

THREE

*W*HAT THE HELL WAS *that?* The question in her mind would have to wait until she found her voice again to ask it. Of course, maybe shapeshifter sex was always that intense. Lou wouldn't know—she hadn't had sex since her transformation. In fact, she hadn't had sex in far too long before that, now that she thought about it.

She thought about the months of celibacy stretching behind her when she could have had him fucking her mindless and wanted to cry at the waste, but she felt too relaxed, too giddy, too . . . drunk. As if the beer and Jell-O shot she'd had in the bar had contained something more potent than alcohol. That should have disturbed her, but she only wanted to roll against him and revel in the sensation of his bare skin against hers and imagine what it would be like to slide against his fur.

Something else should be disturbing her. Ah, yes, the liquid jet when he'd come inside her.

"You didn't use the condom," she said, but it wasn't an accusation. It came out slurred and disinterested.

"Didn't need ribbed or lubricated, did you?" He rubbed his cheek against her hair and then readjusted their position so they lay together spooned on their sides again, with his arms wrapped tight around her. He slid out of her in the process and Lou felt bereft.

"That's so wrong," she protested. "I need you back inside me."

"Told you you'd bitch if I didn't give you at least three orgasms."

He rolled onto his back and positioned her on top of him, facing him. She instantly spread her legs and scooted until the head of his cock nudged her cunt again. He was still thick and engorged, as ready for her as she was for him. With a little wiggle and a shift of angle, she had him sliding into her again. She made a soft sound of satisfaction.

He'd tugged her hair free of her ponytail at some point when she hadn't been paying attention and it fell over her shoulders in a silky slide when she moved. Although she was still wearing her bikini top, and that irritated her.

"Get this top off me," she muttered. "I need to rub my nipples on your chest."

"Your wish is my command." He undid the strings and slipped the top free. Lou closed her eyes in bliss as her bare breasts and her sensitized nipples came into solid contact with heated, male flesh.

She sighed and rubbed her cheek against him, luxuriating in the feel of his body under her. "I want to rub all over you," she told him. "It's like I'm a cat and you're catnip. And I feel drunk. I thought I couldn't get drunk anymore. Tried a couple of times after I started turning furry. Didn't work. Metabolized all the alcohol too fast."

She licked at his skin, tasting the salty tang on her tongue, and wondered why she wanted to fill her mouth with him, wanted every orifice she had to contain him somehow. She mentioned this to him in a drunken slur and felt him finger her ass in response, circling her anus and then sliding a fingertip in.

That was better. His cock hard and thick inside her pussy, his finger teasing her ass. But that still left her mouth. Lou fastened her mouth onto his and sucked his tongue into hers. She wanted to suck his cock, but since she liked it far too much right where it was, she settled for letting him know with little growls and movements that she wanted his tongue fucking her mouth the way his cock was fucking her pussy while his fingertip fucked her ass.

She felt ravenous for him, and the feeling wasn't far removed from the animal bloodlust she'd begun to feel when the full moon approached. The need to hunt, to bring down her prey. Only now it was his sex she craved, and she craved it with her whole being.

And that made her realize that her animal side was rising into ascendance. Soon she wouldn't be able to hold off the change. The only thing keeping her in human form now was the fact that the beast inside her was being satiated by the animalistic mating they were engaged in.

Lou wondered vaguely if the key to werewolf control was sex, if she could balance the beast and the human halves of herself by getting royally laid once a month, but it took too much effort to pursue any logical line of thought so she gave it up and focused on rocking her hips into his, sliding the length of his cock into her sex-starved sheath again and again.

This time it felt different in some way. She still needed his touch, his penetration, but she no longer felt like her skin couldn't contain the force contact between them created. It was still there, an invisible power running from him to her and back like a circuit, but tamer.

When she came again, shuddering and gasping against him, she didn't fear the distant sounds of shattering glass.

Drunk with pleasure and the sheer bliss of contact with him, Lou let herself collapse into him in a boneless heap. She let out a long, soft sigh of contentment.

"Mind if I finish?"

Oh. He was still hard inside her. "G'head," she murmured.

A few hard, quick thrusts and then she felt him spilling himself into her again. Her vaginal walls contracted sharply at the sensation and she quivered with the aftershocks of her orgasm and his.

After a seemingly endless time when she might have dozed, sated with sex and soothed by the rhythmic sounds of the surf and the drone of distant cars on the highway, his voice jolted her back to awareness.

"Okay. Now we need to talk."

FOUR

*H*E WAS PROBABLY RIGHT, Lou mused. Conversations that started out that way weren't likely to end well. And it wasn't just the words *we need to talk* that set her mental alarm stirring. It was the tone of his voice, no longer tinged with laughter or amusement. He meant business now.

Well, all good things had to end. And at least he'd been true to his word and given her three orgasms first. She felt vaguely grateful to him for that even while annoyance at interrupting her post-coital bliss was rising up fast to counter it.

"Right, back to business," she sighed. "You're not the bad guy. I'm not the bad guy. Which means we should probably get dressed and go looking for him now."

"I meant we need to talk about other things," he told her. "Although that's certainly important too. How do you know I'm not the bad guy?"

"Dunno," she said. The line of logic that had told her he wasn't seemed too far away to grasp now. There had been something, though. What? Oh, yes. "You have a sense of humor," she pointed out.

"So do you. In a smart-ass kind of way." He let his hands rove away from her ass, which was unfortunate, and along her spine, which was nice enough that she forgave him. "Anything else?"

"It doesn't add up," she answered. "I figured out why, can't remember now. Gimme a minute."

That made him laugh. "I'll remember this, get you naked and handcuff you anytime I want to distract you. A few good orgasms and you're putty in my hands." He toyed with her hair. "You're not a natural blonde, are you?"

"Not telling." Lou smiled against his bare skin.

"I could make you tell me." One hand slid in between them so he could finger her still-sensitized clit.

Yeah, he certainly could. With that kind of torture, she'd sing like a canary. If she could talk. Problem was, coherent speech didn't really go along with what he was doing to her down there.

"But I'll find out soon enough. First things first. What's your name?"

"Louise. Lou," she clarified, figuring they were on intimate enough terms for him to use her nickname. The formality of having him use her full name after she'd asked him to bang her in the ass while fucking her would seem ludicrous. Not to mention hypocritical.

"Just Lou?"

"Catrell."

"Stuck on keeping the last name? Planning to hyphenate?"

"S' never come up," Lou informed him and wiggled her hips a little to get more pressure on her clit. A fourth orgasm didn't seem like a bad idea. Since she might never get another opportunity to play with him, it seemed only right to enjoy the present to the fullest.

But he was still focused on talking.

"It just did. I'm kind of a traditionalist, myself, always imagined my wife would take my last name. And I'd rather you didn't hyphenate, because that could lead to our kids having four last names someday."

Lou felt her eyes fly open at the implication. "Do you always propose to any girl who lets you handcuff her and do anal play on the first date?"

"We're a little past the proposal stage. We're mated. We consummated the bond. No condom, exchange of body fluids. I figured you'd prefer that to us drawing each other's blood in the act, by the way. For a werewolf, you seem kind of squeamish."

After a frozen moment, Lou discovered that she could in fact leap off him in spite of the handcuffs, the current dysfunctional state of her brain and the handicap of not really wanting to separate herself from his cock, not to mention his talented hands. She hit the sand, rolled and shook her head to clear it.

Clarity did not follow. "What? Excuse me?" she shrieked at him. "Are you saying we're *married*?"

"I asked you if you understood what was happening." He followed her, pinned her in the sand and scowled down at her. "You recognized me as your mate. What, does it mess with your plans that you can't fuck another male as long as I live?"

He didn't seem good-humored now. He seemed extremely pissed. She could feel the wolf inside him rising up and it didn't take much imagination to hear it snarling softly at her.

Whatever this mating business was, she knew instinctively that he was now her alpha as well as her mate and anything he perceived as a threat to deprive him of what he'd claimed territorially was a bad thing. She did not want that kind of a fight with him. Especially since he had the right to claim her, if she understood him correctly.

"Give me a minute," Lou managed to say. "This is a little surprising, okay? I need a moment to adjust. I came here hunting the big bad wolf. I wasn't planning a beachside wedding ceremony. Now you're telling me I just got married wearing nothing but a bikini top, sneakers and handcuffs."

She felt the full impact of that hit her. Then she smacked her head into the sand. Hard. Repeatedly. "Not a Kodak moment. Okay? Most women get apple blossoms, white lace, that kind of thing. And I could be wrong, but I'm pretty sure Jan and Dean never performed 'The Wedding March.'"

"Oh." The tension went out of him. He touched her face lightly. "I can see how this lacks a little in the way of romance from your perspective. We could go to Vegas, have a strictly human ceremony if you like."

"Because getting married to a total stranger in a neon chapel by a guy dressed like Elvis would be so much better? I don't even know your *name*." Lou felt her lips tremble, heard the betraying quaver in her voice and felt tears well up in her eyes. Oh, hell, now she was going to top off the evening by crying like a girl. If she'd spent the last year planning ways to screw tonight up, she couldn't have beat this.

"It's Dylan."

"Dylan," she repeated. She sniffled. "Dylan the werewolf?" That was funny enough to head off the unwanted weeping fit.

"My mom was into poetry," he informed her. "Dylan Thomas, Bob Dylan. I suffered for it. But I didn't get turned into a werewolf until I was eighteen, so it's not like she knew I was going to grow up to lead a wolf pack."

"Guess not. I'm sure my mom never imagined my current life, either."

He bent forward and brushed his lips across hers gently. The kiss was sweet and reassuring. Unrushed, undemanding, it seduced her into wanting more. Only a kiss, but her body flooded with heat while her vaginal walls flooded with liquid and clenched reflexively in anticipation. "There's a human life too."

"Right." Lou thrashed in the sand until she had herself cuddled into Dylan. He accommodated her, wrapping arms and legs around her and snuggling her close. The more of him she was in contact with, the better she felt. Touching him was an irresistible compulsion. It comforted her and made her feel safe. Warm. Secure. Even, weirdly, loved. "How come I want to keep touching you?"

"We're mated. The bond is new. We feed it by touch."

Well, there was an answer. Sort of. But she could find out more about that later. Now it seemed more important to learn a little more about the man she'd gotten herself bound to. "So what are you doing here in California, anyway? You're not from around here."

"I got transferred."

The utter normalcy of that floored her. He had a day job. Chances were, his coworkers had no idea what he did during the full moon.

"Didn't somebody else used to be alpha before you got here?" Lou asked. "What happened, a fight to the death?"

Dylan laughed. "Hardly. He wanted to retire. His mate wanted to move to the Florida Keys to live on a houseboat. So I made them both happy and took over the local pack." He grinned at her. "Not very dramatic."

"And what do you do when you're not howling at the moon?"

"I'm a system administrator."

Lou nodded. "That works. Those guys are all weird, you'd fit right in."

"And what about you? What do you do when you're not picking up strange men in bars?"

"I used to be in insurance claims."

"Used to be?"

"I quit when I realized I wanted to tear my boss's throat out for refusing to cover a kid's cancer treatment." Lou brooded for a moment. "I wasn't sure if I'd actually do it one night when I wasn't exactly myself, so I figured a little distance was in order. And it gave me more time to focus on revenge. You know, hunting down the rabid jerk who turned me into Ms. Most In Need of Electrolysis once a month."

"Ah. So that's how you ended up a werewolf who doesn't know what happens when you meet your mate. You weren't a planned addition to a pack, you were a victim of a rogue attack." He sat up and pulled her upright with him in a fluid motion. "That explains what you were doing in the bar tonight. I thought at first you might've been an accomplice."

"So you handcuffed me and gave me the best sex of my life anyway?"

"He might have coerced you into helping if he was your alpha. So I gave you the opportunity to change allegiances," he explained. "By the time we got to the sex part, I'd figured out you weren't with him. Our wolves recognized each other as mates. Best sex in your life?"

"Maybe only the second best." Lou kept a straight face and gave him a considering look. "Maybe I need another round to see how you rate."

"You're an animal." He gave her a slow, feral smile that told her how much he liked that about her.

"Any time now," Lou agreed. "I can't believe I'm still wearing skin instead of fur. It's late."

"The mating bond," he nodded. "We started in human form, we had to remain in that form until it was complete."

"Isn't it complete now?"

"Yes, but there are aftereffects. Do you actually know anything about werewolves that you didn't learn from comic books or movies?"

"Yeah, I got a real education in an alley one night," she shot back. "Okay, so I'm dumb about the wolf stuff. You can bring me up to speed. It's not like the one who tried to kill me hung around to see if I'd changed and needed a mentor."

"Don't be touchy." He pressed his thumb against her lips in a half-caress, half-silencing gesture. "I should probably mention the no condom thing again now. Most couples hope for pregnancy as a result of the ritual. Children conceived during mating have special abilities. It's considered a blessing on the bonded pair. If I'd realized you didn't know anything, I would have acted differently. I couldn't have stopped, once mates recognize each other mating can't be stopped. But I could've used the condom."

"So I could be knocked up right now and we could be the proud parents of something out of the X-Men? You know, I don't think most one-night stands are this complicated." Lou closed her eyes and buried her face in the curve of his neck.

"It might not happen."

"No, it'd be just my luck to have twins. You haven't even had a chance to see me at my best and you'll be watching me hurl for the next nine months, blowing up like a blimp and then screaming through labor. Just what every fledgling relationship needs."

Dylan scooped her into his lap and placed a kiss on top of her bleached-blond hair. "On the bright side, this is truly 'til death do us part. I'll never desire any other female above you. I wouldn't leave you. And we'll never stop needing to touch each other, although in a week or so we'll be able to leave each other long enough to go about a normal life, going to work, that kind of thing. But mates don't separate, not without becoming seriously weakened, and if it goes on too long it's fatal."

"So no going home to Mother if I get mad at you."

"Nope. We fight it out and stay together." He nuzzled her playfully. "And then we have make-up sex."

"Which the twins will interrupt just when it's getting good."

"Are you always this grumpy? Or are you still pissed about getting married in nothing but sneakers and handcuffs?"

"And a bikini top," Lou reminded him. "I think that adds a touch of class."

"I need a real answer here." He tipped her chin up and made eye contact. "I need to know you don't regret this. My entire adult life I've known the wolf in me would recognize my mate. It's something I accepted long ago. To resist is to fight against your own nature. That doesn't happen often among us, but when it does, the results are unhappy to say the least. It's not enough that you belong to me now. I need you to want to be mine. I want all of you."

And the weird part was, she believed him. Maybe it was another effect of their mating, maybe it created a sort of emotional resonance or empathy, because she could feel the tension in him, feel him willing her to want him, to . . . love him.

It mattered to him that she was there willingly, that she wanted to be his and that he would hold her heart as well as her body.

Their wolves had recognized each other as mates, he'd said. And in the past year she'd learned to trust her wolf self. It had never led her wrong. It frequently led her away from trouble her human self would never have seen coming.

She'd known him for only a few hours.

She was probably certifiably insane.

But she was pretty sure she did, in fact, love him. The term he'd used, recognition, really did describe what she felt. It was as if her wolf self recognized him, remembered him and was making her human body and her heart remember too. Almost as if they'd known each other before in some other realm, where they'd run together under a distant sky, hunted together, depended on each other, mated for all time.

Lou opened her mouth to tell him what he needed to hear, but before she could, an inhuman howl split the night.

FIVE

THEY'VE SPOTTED HIM," DYLAN said. He reached for his jeans, retrieved the key to the handcuffs and freed her. "My pack's been watching this place, waiting for him. We can't allow a rogue to go free, and we can't leave him to human justice. Stay here. I'll call you when it's safe."

Call her when it was safe? Leave her behind while the men took care of business? That seemed like a bad precedent. But he slid into his jeans and vanished into the darkness before she could argue with him.

"Dammit," Lou muttered. She groped in the sand for her bikini, found it and scrambled into it. All she needed to do now was retrieve her gun to complete the Terminator Barbie look.

How was Dylan planning to take the bad guy out, anyway? He wasn't armed. She would have smelled the gun oil if he'd had one, which was why she'd left hers in the car. She knew she wouldn't have a chance of getting up close and personal with the big, bad wolf without him knowing she was packing and she'd needed to appear helpless to attract him. The gun would have given away the game. Since killing his victims in their cars seemed like his favorite way to get his jollies, hiding the gun in her glove box had struck Lou as the perfect solu-tion.

Oh, shit. Dylan was going to fight him. Lou felt icy fear prickle along her spine. And he might not be able to shift yet because of the aftereffects holding their transformation off. He might even now be facing a rogue werewolf in his too-vulnerable human form.

She retrieved her jacket with the car keys and ran to her car, grateful every step of the way for the strength and speed she'd gained along with her wolf self. If she'd been merely human, she wouldn't have been fast enough. She reached the car, shoved in the key and turned it just as the sounds of fighting reached her ears. One punch on the button to her glove box and then the Springfield Armory compact was in her hand. She grabbed it and checked the chamber as she ran to make sure the round was still there. Counting the round in the chamber, she had eight shots. It would have to be enough.

Of course, if eight .45 caliber hollow-point rounds didn't stop the rogue werewolf, finding more bullets would be the least of their problems. Lou refused to think that she'd be such a rotten shot at the critical moment that all eight bullets would miss. Her new abilities included better than human vision and reflexes. Her aim had been honed on the practice range until she was confident in her ability to shoot straight when the target was moving, and accuracy and speed mattered.

I won't miss, she chanted silently while she ran. *I'll nail that bastard and Dylan will be fine. He won't be hurt.* And then added in a silent prayer for help to any power listening, *please.*

Lou could hear them before she could see them, her sensitive ears locating sources of movement in the night. She could only hope the good guys wouldn't think she was part of the problem and attack her while she found a place to take aim.

Then she could see them, her mate and the rogue. Two massive wolves locked in combat while the other weres ranged around them. Maybe it was an aftereffect of mating, but she knew Dylan even in his wolf form instantly. He'd been able to shift, after all, while she remained locked in human form. Maybe because he was stronger than she was, maybe because he knew more than she did or had better control. Whatever the reason, she was grateful for her hands and more aware than ever of the urgent need to use them before they turned to paws.

The combatants tumbled together, a flurry of snapping jaws and lightning-fast movements. No clear shot. She couldn't be sure she wouldn't hit Dylan until they separated.

The rogue wolf was huge, powerful and not bound by any sense of decency to fight fair or any hesitation to do mortal injury. And Lou doubted he was burdened much by sanity. Given the abnormal feats of strength an insane human was capable of, what could an insane werewolf do? She didn't doubt Dylan's strength or agility, but she also didn't trust anything short of a silver bullet to stop this monster. Fear for her mate rose up but she ruthlessly forced it down. No time for that now. Now what mattered was watching for her moment and taking it when it came.

Dylan broke free for an instant and whirled to take a new angle of attack. The rogue followed, but it was all the opportunity she needed, a clear shot with no other werewolves behind him. That mattered. The hollow-point bullets would stop on impact, but the silver filling they carried was another story. There was a risk the silver would continue on through the body and out the other side, endangering any werewolf unlucky enough to get in the way. Lou aimed for his head, told herself she was just at the range shooting another practice target and pulled the trigger.

The sound hurt her ears but she didn't flinch. She kept the gun steady and followed the first shot with the rest of the clip in rapid succession.

She didn't miss. The rogue werewolf shifted into a naked man as he fell to the ground.

"Eat silver, you bastard," Lou said out loud in satisfaction. "I might have learned about werewolves from comic books and movies, but they got that part right."

Then she dropped the gun and ran to her mate.

She got a fierce growl instead of thanks.

"Yes, I know. I was supposed to wait." She flung her arms around Dylan's neck and hugged him to her, needing the contact to reassure herself that he was unhurt. "You should know right from the start that I'm not going to sit back and twiddle my thumbs like some useless decoration when you need me."

Then the transfiguring touch of the full moon told Lou that the time for words had ended. Tomorrow they could talk again.

She shifted into her second form while Dylan waited. Then they ran together in the night, running for the sheer physical joy of it, side by side, pacing each other, sharing the wild night that stretched out before them, and it was like coming home.

"SO YOU'RE NOT A natural blonde."

The teasing words chased away the last remnants of sleep. Lou came awake and turned her head to find the speaker. She opened her eyes to see a pair of amber eyes gazing down at her. Laugh lines crinkled in the corners, deepened by the satisfied smile that currently filled Dylan's face. He was obviously pleased with himself for guessing right.

She vaguely remembered that they'd made their way to his home in the predawn dark and fallen into bed together as they shifted back to human form. By the angle of the sun streaming through the window, she guessed it was close to noon now.

"Nope," Lou agreed, smiling back at him. "Clairol trumps Mother Nature."

"Want to tell me where you got silver bullets? You can't just buy those off the shelf."

"Nope," she said again. "And even asking questions about them will get you some pretty strange looks, in case you wondered. Amazing how anybody wanting to know about silver bullets comes off as a whack job." She reached out to touch his bare chest, letting her hand trail down to his abdomen in a lingering caress. The need to touch him would probably lessen over time, but she didn't think it would ever go away. "I settled for regular hollow-points and filled them with silver myself. Very carefully."

"Effective." Dylan captured her wayward hand with one of his and carried it to his mouth. He pressed a kiss into her palm. "You're a good shot too. Remind me not to piss you off."

"Don't piss me off," Lou said, fighting the urge to giggle. One night with him and she felt downright lighthearted, happy, buoyant. Pissed off seemed like an impossibility at the moment.

"But as the alpha around here, if you disobey me again you'll find yourself back in handcuffs."

"Promises, promises."

Lou was pretty sure he'd keep them though. And was looking forward to it.